Framing Freedom
A Journey Through the Lens

Susie Bennett

Copyright © Susie Bennett 2025

The moral right of this author has been asserted.

All rights reserved.

All characters and events in this publication, other than those clearly in the public domain, are fictitious and any resemblance to real persons, living or dead, is purely coincidental.

No part of this publication may be reproduced, stored in a retrieval system, or transmitted, in any form or by any means, without the prior permission in writing of the publisher, nor be otherwise circulated in any form of binding or cover other than that in which it is published and without a similar condition including this condition being imposed on the subsequent purchaser.

Design, typesetting and publishing by UK Book Publishing

www.ukbookpublishing.com

ISBN: 978-1-917329-51-4

Framing Freedom

A Journey Through the Lens

INTRODUCTION

In "Framing Freedom: A Journey Through the Lens," Lara Hargrove, a spirited young woman in a wheelchair, embarks on an adventure of a lifetime, armed with her camera and a determination to capture the world's beauty. With the charming local guide Finn O'Reilly by her side, they traverse picturesque landscapes and uncover hidden gems, igniting Lara's passion for exploration.

Evelyn Baxter, Lara's witty best friend, offers artistic support, helping to frame stunning photographs that tell their story. Along the way, they meet Theo Marquez, a mysterious wildlife photographer whose skills deepen Lara's connection to nature. Nadia Thompson, a compassionate travel journalist, mentors her, sharing poignant insights into the magic that lies beyond the lens.

Lara's thirst for adventure leads her to the eccentric Jasper Woodson, who spins tales of the past, and the adrenaline-fuelled Scarlett Rivers, whose daring spirit propels Lara into exhilarating challenges. With Emilio Cruz's custom camera rig and Maya Patel's environmental cause, Lara learns to intertwine photography with advocacy. Guided by the historian Archie Bramwell, they delve into ancient ruins, uncovering lost stories. Through laughter, challenges, and breathtaking moments, Lara discovers that true freedom lies not just in adventures, but in the stories they create.

FRAMING FREEDOM: A JOURNEY THROUGH THE LENS

In a world brimming with beauty and untold stories, Lara Hargrove rolls into an adventure that will forever alter her perception of freedom. Confined to a wheelchair but never to her dreams, she wields her camera like a key that unlocks the captivating wonders of life. Join Lara as she journeys through vibrant landscapes, where she meets the charismatic Finn O'Reilly, who reveals hidden gems pulsating with life and history.

Together, they forge a path filled with laughter, support, and unexpected friendships. With each click of her camera, Lara unveils new perspectives alongside Evelyn, her fiercely loyal best friend, while mysterious mentor Nadia fills her with wisdom about the magic waiting in the world beyond the lens. Guided by the tales of eccentric Jasper and the daring spirit of adventurers like Scarlett, Lara learns that every picture tells a story—one that can challenge perception and inspire change.

As she captures the essence of nature with Theo, and explores the ecological connections with Maya, Lara discovers that freedom does not merely lie in the landscapes she traverses but in the profound narratives she weaves and the vibrant colours of life she brings to light. This is more than just a journey; it is a testament to the indomitable spirit of adventure, where every frame taken echoes the voice of liberation.

THE FRAMING OF DREAMS: A WORLD AWAITS

The soft murmur of the seaside was a symphony of freedom that danced through the air, coaxing Lara Hargrove from her slumber. The sun peeked through the gossamer curtains of her room, illuminating her faded posters of travel destinations that adorned the walls like a gallery of dreams. Today, everything felt different; it was the day she would venture into the world beyond her confines with her beloved camera, the instrument through which she intended to explore life's myriad hues.

As her fingers glided over the weathered strap of the camera, memories flickered like snapshots in her mind. It had been a gift from Evelyn, her best friend, who had promised her an adventure that was both thrilling and transformative. Together they had poured countless hours into planning their escapade, mapping out milestones that included places painted in vibrant colours, textured with tales of adventure waiting to be uncovered.

"Ready to make some memories?" Evelyn bounded into the room, her eyes alight with enthusiasm. She carried a rucksack filled with not just photography gear, but excitement and cheer–everything Lara needed to step outside of her bubble.

"Always," Lara replied with a soft smile, her spirit unshaken by her physical constraints. With a final check of her camera settings, she wheeled herself towards the door, the moment bursting with potential, as though the world outside had conspired to welcome her with open arms.

The fresh, salty breeze welcomed them as they rolled outside, with the rhythmic lapping of waves setting a backdrop that pulled Lara in. Finn O'Reilly, the local guide with auburn hair and a boyish grin, stood waiting as if he had just stepped out from the pages of one of her adventure novels.

"Welcome to your new playground!" he said, his voice smooth as honey. "Are you ready to explore some hidden gems?"

"Absolutely!" Lara replied, buoyed by the sheer enthusiasm shimmering in the air.

THE FRAMING OF DREAMS: A WORLD AWAITS

Finn led them down winding paths through the coastal town, narrating stories that adorned the landscape like embellishments in a piece of art. As he pointed out the unique flora and fauna of the region, Evelyn snapped shots of everything, while Lara focused on Finn's storytelling. The way he spoke about the wilds tinged her world with possibilities.

"If you stand right there," Finn instructed, gesturing to a particularly striking dappled sunlight filtering through the branches of a gnarled tree, "you can capture the essence of nature at its finest."

Lara savoured his words, composing the scene in her mind even before clicking the shutter. This wasn't merely photography; it was an adventure into the heart of existence itself. She breathed deeply, gleaning freedom through each frame she captured, each picture a testament to experiences beyond her grasp.

Later, they discovered Jasper Woodson, an eccentric old man who had carved a niche in the quiet village they now explored. His home, an eclectic sanctuary of wandering stories and aged wood, brimmed with memorabilia from his rambles.

"Every rustle in the leaves has a story," he told them as he accompanied Lara and Evelyn through his garden filled with wildflowers. "And every wanderer must listen."

"Do the flowers speak?" Lara asked, intrigued.

"Ah, they don't speak in words," Jasper mused, scratching his beard. "They speak in colours, scents, and the whispers of the breeze. Just like your camera, they frame their stories. You must simply learn to listen."

The wisdom hung in the air with palpable weight, compelling Lara to dig deeper into the world around her. She pondered how each photograph could serve not just as a visual narrative but as a connection between her experiences and those who gazed upon her shots.

As they prepared to leave Jasper's garden, Evelyn playfully threw her arms skyward, her laughter breaking the spell of seriousness. The crisp air filled with their joy, and recognizing the essence of adventure, they posed for a group photo, a moment immortalised in time–all smiles, all friendship, dancing with the light.

The days melted into each other as Lara, Evelyn, and Finn traversed beaches and rugged hills, their encounters laced with spontaneity and laughter. Yet, it was one evening, as dusk painted the sky in swathes of pink and purple, that they met Theo Marquez, a wandering artist who had been capturing the essence of wildlife through his lens for years.

"Are you ready to go wild?" he asked in a soft voice, his gaze flitting between the trees surrounding the clearing. He intrigued Lara, exuding an aura of charm mixed with an underlying mystery.

"I'd love to see the wild world," she said, her heart beating faster at the thought. "What do you recommend?"

"Follow the light, and let the wild reveal itself to you. It's all around if you're willing to be still and observe," Theo advised, a grin dancing on his lips.

As they set out that night, the forest came alive; dusk settled like a gentle blanket, unveiling surprises at every turn. Lara found herself captivated by the glint of fireflies illuminating the canvas of night, their erratic movements echoing heartbeats in the darkness. She photographed them, creating luminescent snapshots against their dark backdrop, a visual dichotomy between wild chaos and serene beauty.

With each click, she relinquished her fears and insecurities, allowing her camera to narrate the freedom she craved. At that moment, beneath the stars, she felt a profound connection not only to the nature around her but also to the visions that obscured her mind. Each shot whispered promises of uncharted territories ahead.

Days passed, each adventure deepening her yearning for exploration. With Evelyn's artistic support—guiding her on how best to frame each photograph—Lara built a marvellous portfolio that told their stories through dynamic moments and vulnerable perspectives. But as they sat on the edge of a cliff overlooking the ocean one evening, a thought bubbled up within her.

"Why isn't this a career? Why do we feel confined by ideas of what photography should be?" She looked out at the horizon, seeking answers in the swirls of clouds.

"Maybe," Evelyn pondered, tapping her chin, "it's because no one dares to break the boundaries we set ourselves. We create these frames, but it's essential to explore beyond them."

With those words igniting a spark in her heart, Lara knew the journey was just beginning. She sought out fresh perspectives, not just limiting her subjects to landscapes, but also delving into the rich tapestry of lives existing parallel to her own, a synergy she hoped would resonate through her art.

In pursuit of this new vision, they met Nadia Thompson, a travel journalist whose heart radiated warmth. Intrigued by Lara's initiative, she took it upon herself to mentor the young photographer.

"Your voice matters, Lara," she guided. "Let your photos be a conduit for stories that must be told."

The network of creative minds around Lara grew, each influencing her journey. She found camaraderie with Scarlett Rivers, the extreme sports enthusiast whose fearlessness breathed new life into her daring pursuits. "Why not capture the exuberance of adventure?" Scarlett challenged one afternoon, her energetic disposition contagious.

With each meeting and unforgettable experience, Lara's lens opened; she began viewing her world through an array of filters—each unique and expressive. Emilio Cruz, a tech-savvy inventor, gifted Lara with a custom camera rig that elevated her perspective, allowing her to capture dynamic shots she'd only ever dreamt of.

"Now," he declared as he presented the device, "you can roll front row at life's adventures."

"Let's chase some adrenaline!" she exclaimed, the thrill of new possibilities surging through her.

Amid this whirlwind of encouragement and creativity, Lara's quest had evolved into something greater—it was an empowering venture, an odyssey to embrace the world around her while uncovering threads of her spirit. Each photo snapped enriched her understanding of beauty, freedom, and connection.

As she returned to her favourite cliff, the waves crashing against the rocks below, Lara accepted the fact that her journey was never about the photos themselves; rather, it was about taking full ownership of her narrative, framing her existence through the lens of her camera.

No longer merely a spectator of life, she was part of a grander story, each click reverberating with the pulse of a world waiting to be framed.

In that moment of clarity, she realised the world awaited, and she was finally ready to embrace the freedom it offered—one frame at a time.

THROUGH THE LENS OF LIMITATION

Lara Hargrove gazed through the viewfinder of her camera, the world around her transformed into a vivid tapestry of colours and shapes. The gardens of the quaint village, bursting with life, were her canvas, each blossom a potential masterpiece awaiting her keen eye. Seated in her wheelchair, the familiar pang of limitation flickered in the back of her mind, but today, she was fuelled by an undying spirit. Adventure was calling, and she was ready to answer.

"From this angle, the light will bathe the flowers beautifully," Evelyn Baxter chimed in, adjusting her own camera. Her cheeky grin sparked encouragement as she perched next to Lara. "Just wait till you edit these; they'll be stunning!"

Together, they had made plans to explore a hidden meadow Finn O'Reilly had mentioned, a place so captivating that it seemed to radiate magic.

With Finn's gentle guidance, their journey promised discovery, but Lara felt the weight of uncertainty. What if they encountered uneven terrain? Would she be able to navigate?

"Don't think about it too much, Lara," Evelyn said, reading her thoughts like an open book. "We'll cross that bridge when we get to it. This is about seeing differently."

A soft breeze ruffled the hair on her forehead as Finn approached, his infectious enthusiasm tangible in the air. "Ready for a mini-adventure?" He placed a hand on Lara's shoulder, igniting a fire of excitement. In his presence, her worries danced away. The vibrant hues of the flowers shimmered in her vision—every detail sharpening, intensifying her resolve.

As they made their way to the meadow, Finn spun stories of the area, filling the quiet with history and folklore. Every word painted a scene, and his passion enveloped them like a warm embrace. "You know," he said, glancing back at Lara, "there's this old tree at the meadow's edge. Rumour has it that if you wish upon its branches, magic happens."

Lara smiled, a lovely vision blooming in her imagination. She might not leap over streams or climb mountains, but with Finn guiding her, she felt every bit the adventurer she had always imagined being. Far from limited, her world was expanding—each click of the shutter capturing not just moments, but emotions, laughter, and friendships intertwined.

They reached the meadow, a sprawling sea of wildflowers dancing in the sun, an ethereal beauty that stirred a longing in Lara's heart. She could already feel the nature beckoning, a symphony of colours around her. But as Finn began guiding her across the uneven ground, a knot of anxiety tightened in her chest. "What if I can't make it through this?" she whispered, the fear bubbling to the surface.

"You're doing splendidly!" Finn reassured her, guiding the wheelchair with deft movements. "Embrace the adventure! Everyone has limitations; it's what you do with them that counts."

Evelyn's laughter chimed in, lifting the despair. "We're all a little broken in one way or another. Sometimes, that just makes us more interesting!"

Giggling, Lara pressed on, each roll of the wheels a declaration of her strength. If the world around her could dazzle in its imperfections, so could she. The uneven patches became opportunities for growth, each bump a reminder that her journey was uniquely hers.

Once settled in the meadow, Lara paused and surveyed the scene, the gentle rustle of leaves intertwined with the buzzing of bees. She drew in a breath and raised her camera. Suddenly, everything crystallised—the blossoms bobbing at the edges of her frame, the vivid blue sky above. The click of the shutter resonated like a heartbeat, each photograph becoming a testament of beauty captured amidst limitation.

Hours passed in a haze of laughter and artistry as Lara explored the meadow's treasures alongside Evelyn. They shared tips and exchanged creative ideas while capturing the essence of every flower and insect. At one point, Finn captured a fleeting moment of joy. "Look at that butterfly!" he pointed. "It's dancing just for you!"

Lara turned her camera toward the creature, heart racing as she focused. Click. Another moment, preserved. She felt a euphoric freedom, each frame echoing the possibility of countless others outside her own confines.

As the sun dipped lower, casting a golden hue across the meadow, Theo Marquez, the enigmatic wildlife photographer, drifted into view. With his wild, unkempt hair and piercing gaze, he seemed as much a part of nature as the trees themselves. The spark of curiosity ignited in Lara, captivated by him and the way he moved through the world.

"Hey there," he said with a gentle tilt of his head, his voice smooth like the flowing river. "Mind if I join you?"

"Sure," Lara replied, excitement bubbling inside. "What brings you here?"

"I heard the evening light was magical, and I couldn't resist capturing it," he said, revealing a canvas bag of photography gear. "You're working the scene beautifully, though. Mind sharing your secret?"

Suddenly, Lara felt empowered, her camera transforming into a bridge, connecting them. "It's all about finding the best perspectives, I suppose. I think limitations, in some ways, help us see the world differently."

Theo smiled, a knowing look glimmering in his eyes. "That's a profound thought. It reminds me of a quote I once heard: 'A photographer can see the world without restraints, even when life places them.' You capture beauty even in limitation, and that's a valuable skill."

When Theo shared technics on focusing on movement in photography, Lara's eyes sparkled with recognition. Each suggestion he offered sparked inspiration, igniting scenes within her mind. They spent the golden hour sharing techniques and stories, Lara absorbing every word like a sponge.

As they packed up after an enthralling day, Finn, Evelyn, and Theo helped Lara navigate the path back through the meadow. "Today was incredible!" Evelyn exclaimed, joy radiating from her as she reviewed the photos they had taken. "We've captured magic in every frame!"

They all clapped and honked their cameras together, thrilling to the idea of adventures that awaited them ahead. Lara's heart swelled, buoyed by friendship and the realisation that these moments were framed within a broader canvas filled with love and experiences.

As evening fell, darkness began to tinge the edges of the horizon. A soft sense of nostalgia washed over Lara, one that came with the promise of tomorrow's adventures. That was the thing about limitations– they often led to the most unexpected of journeys.

"One more thing," Theo said as they walked under the stars. "You should never underestimate the beauty of where you come from."

Lara considered his words, realising that limitations did not define her; they merely shaped her into a burgeoning artist with unique perspectives. Finishing off the day, laughter and stories twinkled like stars above them, blending beautifully with the richness of the earth beneath her wheels.

With the world framed around her through the lens of her camera, Lara Hargrove embraced limitation not as a prison, but as a gateway to freedom. And with every shutter click, she felt herself soar.

THE FIRST SNAP: CAPTURING A MOMENT

The sun hung low over the horizon, casting a warm, golden hue over the rugged terrain. Lara Hargrove adjusted the strap of her camera, her heart racing with anticipation. Every corner of the world seemed to whisper secrets, and she was determined to capture them. Today, she and Finn O'Reilly were exploring the labyrinthine paths that wound through the village, each leading to untold stories waiting to be discovered.

"Are you ready for an adventure?" Finn's cheerful voice broke through her thoughts. His dark curls bounced as he grinned, the sunlight catching the warmth of his smile.

"Absolutely! But you'd better keep up," Lara replied, her spirits soaring as she wheeled herself closer to him.

As they ventured deeper into the village, Finn guided her to a narrow alleyway framed by crumbling stone walls and vibrant splashes of bougainvillea. Lara's camera hung like a lifeline around her neck, poised to frame the moment.

"Take a look at that," Finn said, pointing to a dusty mural adorning the wall, depicting a flourishing village life from decades ago.

Lara manoeuvred herself into the perfect position, the aperture of her lens opening wide as she focused. As she clicked the shutter, she felt a rush of exhilaration; the mural seemed to transform with each frame clicked, infusing new life into its faded pigments.

"Look at that! You captured its spirit!" Finn exclaimed, leaning closer. He examined the screen: the colours seemed to pulsate, revealing the rich heritage woven within the strokes of every brush.

"Right? It's stunning how a perspective can reveal so much depth," Lara said, eager to delve deeper into her newfound passion.

Together, they continued, the air thick with the scents of spices and freshly baked bread wafting from nearby stalls. They paused at Jasper Woodson's little shop, a treasure trove of vintage cameras and adorned trinkets. The old man's voice was like wind chimes dancing in the breeze.

THE FIRST SNAP: CAPTURING A MOMENT

"Ah, you've come to learn of the tales these walls could tell!" Jasper grinned as they entered.

Lara's eyes sparkled. What stories lay behind the dusty lenses and weathered notebooks?

"Every camera is a time machine," Jasper continued, his voice deep and resonant. "Each shot freezes a moment in time, capturing not just the image, but the essence of the experience."

Lara felt a spark ignite within her. "What if we could capture the essence of life in the village?" she pondered aloud.

Jasper's eyes lit up. "Exactly! Life is full of hidden perspectives just waiting to be uncovered. Even in this very damn village." He waved his hand towards the window. "You might find that with the right angle, beauty is everywhere."

Encouraged by Jasper's words, Lara and Finn set off again, Lara wheeling down the alley, eager to explore every hidden nook. Evelyn Baxter, her ever-encouraging best friend, had always said the magic of photography lay in discovering which moments to frame. With each snap, Lara felt her confidence blossoming.

They stumbled upon a quiet courtyard, petals from a cherry blossom tree raining gently around them. Lara shifted her camera to capture Finn, clad in his earnest enthusiasm, surrounded by the flurry of pink. The world stood still as she framed the shot, feeling the stark contrast between nature and humanity.

"Hey, what about me?" Evelyn's laughter echoed from behind them. She had joined them, her camera poised at the ready as she caught a flurry of candid moments between Lara and Finn.

"Let's create our own story!" Evelyn suggested excitedly, suggesting they take turns photographing one another.

Lara turned her attention to Evie as they rotated through their group, the trio weaving an unspoken language with each shutter click; they danced around frames and perspectives, every shot revealing more than just faces, but emotions etched in the capture of fleeting seconds.

Just then, a figure caught Lara's eye—a tall, enigmatic man sketching underneath a tree, surrounded by a collection of photographs of wildlife. Curious, she wheeled closer, peering over at the intricate strokes of his pencil against the aged paper.

"Who's that?" she asked Finn.

"That's Theo Marquez. A brilliant photographer who spends his time chasing the wild," Finn said, admiration evident in his voice. "He travels far and wide to capture nature in its most untamed form."

THE FIRST SNAP: CAPTURING A MOMENT

Feeling the tug of curiosity and inspiration, Lara called out to him as he looked up, his dark eyes clashing with her cheering curiosity. "Excuse me! Can we see what you've captured?"

Theo smiled, a hint of intrigue in his gaze. "Sure," he replied, motioning for them to come closer. "Photography finds its magic in perspective. What do you see when you look through the lens?"

As Lara observed Theo's photographs, her breath caught in her throat. Captured in full frame were expansive landscapes, intimate moments of animals living out their wild lives.

"It's about patience and waiting for that perfect moment," Theo explained as he noticed her mesmerised expression. "Just like the cherry blossoms... capturing the profound beauty within chaos," he gestured towards an image of a fox framed by autumn leaves. "What do you think?"

"It's incredible," Lara breathed, inspired anew. The idea that photography could transcend mere images to become storytelling struck her deeply. "Every photo tells a story... it's about finding that hidden perspective."

"Exactly," Theo affirmed, a smile creeping across his face. "You're already on the right path, Lara. Just remember that sometimes the best stories are found off the beaten track."

With renewed zeal, Lara took to the streets again, deeper into the portions of the village where few dared to venture, searching for those hidden gems that Theo had encouraged her to find.

They arrived at a weathered bridge, casting a reflection upon the calm water below. Finn leaned over the railing, his excitement infectious, inspiring Lara to shoot from below the bridge's arches, her camera pressed against the cool stone.

"You've got to see this!" he called to her, waving at something beneath the water's surface.

Lara shifted her position and clicked the shutter. The ripples created shapes that danced together—an abstract painting in motion. The frame melted into a compelling image—both serene and dynamic.

"Your photos reflect a fantastic perspective," Evelyn chimed in, peering over at Lara's screen, delight lighting her features.

"Take it a step further," Finn encouraged. "Let's keep pushing ourselves and our creativity!"

They paused for a moment, breathing in the magic of the day's flotilla of unfolding creativity. Just then, the unmistakable sound of skateboard wheels rolling against cobblestones drew their attention.

A bold girl, dressed in vivid colours and radiating confidence, skated past, twirling effortlessly before stopping near them.

THE FIRST SNAP: CAPTURING A MOMENT

"Hey, you lot want to shoot something exhilarating?!" Scarlett Rivers exclaimed, her vibrant energy like an adrenaline shot.

Lara's eyes widened with excitement. "That's exactly what we've been searching for! Show us what you've got!"

With her daring spirit, Scarlett launched into an array of stunts, effortlessly slicing through the air on her skateboard. Lara's fingers flew across the camera's shutter, trying to capture each twist and turn, each act of bravery calling to her adventurous spirit.

"What a perfect angle!" Finn called out, encouraging Scarlett to push her limits.

Under the lens, Lara saw it—the beautiful essence of freedom, the thrill of defiance, the embodiment of life unbound.

As night began to fall, the village turned into a canvas of glowing lights, and the trio settled on a charming terrace overlooking the townsfolk below. They shared stories—Lara about the hidden perspectives she had begun to grasp, Evelyn reflecting on the artistic flair that interwove with every click, and Finn creating a narrative filled with breathing life and adventure.

By the time the stars began to twinkle above, Lara realised that she had uncovered more than just hidden perspectives through her lens; it was a deeper understanding of life itself–the overwhelming beauty in every shadow, the untold stories wrapped within coiled streets, and the connections that lifted her world beyond borders.

With her camera resting beside her, Lara felt the artist in her awaken. Each click echoed echoes of laughter, courage, and love. In that moment, she understood that every photograph they took was not just a frame, but an adventure waiting to unfold.

"Let's do it all again tomorrow!" she exclaimed enthusiastically, and with nodding heads and glinting eyes, they all agreed.

Tomorrow would bring new perspectives and even more adventures, and with her camera in hand, Lara was ready to explore everything the world had to offer.

UNCOVERING HIDDEN PERSPECTIVES

The sun hung low in the sky, casting a golden glow over the quaint village of Eldermoor. The vibrant hues of the sunset painted the sky, creating an ethereal backdrop for Lara Hargrove's first solo photography session. With her trusty camera strapped securely on her lap, she felt an unmistakable thrill coursing through her veins. This moment was not just about the pictures; it was about freedom—her freedom.

"Alright, Lara!" shouted Finn O'Reilly, his warm smile radiating confidence. He leaned against a wooden fence, the charm of a local guide evident in his easy mannerisms. "Let's find the perfect shot! Those hills won't capture themselves."

Lara grinned back, her heart quickening. Finn had been instrumental in coaxing her out of her comfort zone. With his knack for storytelling and keen eye for beauty, he guided her towards hidden gems that even the locals often overlooked. Today, they'd set their sights on the outskirts of the village, where wildflowers danced in the gentle breeze, and the landscape unfolded like a vibrant tapestry.

As she manoeuvred her wheelchair along the narrow path, the air thick with the heady scent of blooming lilacs, Lara's spirit soared. This was the essence of life, of adventure—the whispers of the world beckoning her to discover their secrets.

"Can we stop over there?" Lara pointed excitedly to a clearing where lavender blossoms sprawled in riotous colours. The flowers had a way of capturing light that she felt was worth documenting.

"Of course! The lavender is exquisite at this time of day." Finn motioned with an inviting gesture. They rolled closer to the field, and Lara tilted her head back, allowing the symphony of colours before her to envelop her senses.

As she settled her camera against her chest, she adjusted the carabineer that held it steady. "Evelyn would love this," she mused aloud, envisioning her best friend diving into the scene with fresh ideas and laughter. Evelyn's artistic flair often transformed mundane moments into visual poetry, and Lara felt grateful for their shared experiences.

"Ready?" Finn asked, his enthusiasm infectious. He held his hands out in a dramatic flourish, drawing in a deep breath as if to prepare for an unveiling.

"Definitely!" Lara focused her camera, and suddenly, the world around her transformed. The distant hum of life faded, and all that remained were the wildflowers and the soft, golden light cascading over their petals.

"Just be yourself, Lara," Finn called, his voice a soothing hum in the backdrop. "This isn't just about the shot; it's about what you feel when you press that button."

Nodding, she straightened her back, her fingers poised delicately over the shutter release as she closed one eye to examine the frame through her lens. With that single adjustment, the world narrowed, revealing a captivating scene—delicate blossoms brushing against each other, their vivid colours competing for attention like eager dancers upon a stage.

Lara inhaled the warm air, letting it fill her lungs, and then exhaled slowly, finding her rhythm among the rustling petals. She gently pressed the shutter and, for a fleeting moment, time ceased to exist. The click reverberated in her chest, echoing the thrill of capturing a unique moment—a fragment of beauty that would never be replicated.

"Got it!" Lara exclaimed, a vibrant smile painting her face.

Finn leaned over her shoulder, peering at the image displayed on her camera. "It's stunning! The way the light hits the flowers, it's almost magical."

As they continued their exploration, Lara felt invigorated, her previous doubts about her abilities fading like shadows in the afternoon sun. Each snap was another brushstroke on the vast canvas of her journey. She could hear Evelyn's voice alongside her, critiquing and cheering at once, reminding her to not just capture images, but to capture feelings.

"Look!" Finn pointed excitedly to a stone bridge arching gracefully over a small creek. "We have to shoot there; it's one of the village's hidden gems!"

"Let's go!" Lara responded, her heart racing at the thought of another breathtaking composition. With Finn guiding her towards the weathered stones, she marvelled at how the sunlight danced off the water's surface, creating an enchanting sparkle that glinted like jewels.

As they arrived at the bridge, the gentle gurgling of water provided a soothing soundtrack. Lara positioned herself at an angle that framed the textured stones contrasting against the reflections rippling below. The intricacies of nature began to pull at her— the more she searched, the more she discovered.

"Can you see that?" Finn pointed towards the far side of the bridge where a lone duck glided gracefully across the surface of the stream. "That's a moment waiting for you to capture!"

Following his gaze, Lara's heart flipped at the thought of immortalising life in motion. She adjusted the settings on her camera, her nimble fingers deftly selecting the right adjustments.

"Just breathe," she whispered to herself, closing her eyes for a heartbeat before snapping her thoughts into focus. She felt a rush of energy surge through her, filling her with the determination to encapsulate that tranquil scene.

With a steady hand, she aimed at the duck, the sound of the shutter captivating her spirit. The duck's reflection shimmered upon the water, creating a double dream within a single frame. Each click of the camera became a tiny act of liberation.

Snapping away, she was only partially aware of Finn's presence as he moved about the bridge, immersed in his own story, but she could hear him narrating tales woven into the very fabric of the village—they played in the background like soothing music, enhancing the magic of the moment.

"You're a natural!" Finn shouted over, his encouragement lifting her spirits even higher.

"This is exhilarating!" Lara shouted back. "I never thought I'd feel so alive just by capturing moments!"

As the sun began to sink below the horizon, she felt an overwhelming need to capture everything—the warmth of the glow enveloping her, the way the light blended into the shadows, and the quiet murmur of the creek inviting calming thoughts. She turned her camera inward, capturing her own reflection in the water.

"What do you see?" Finn's voice broke through her musings, rooting her back to reality.

"Just... everything," Lara replied, feeling the words spill from her. "I see myself finally stepping into the light."

She looked at Finn, a tear glistening in her eye. The first snap had opened up a world she had only imagined. Behind the lens, she found not only beauty but an unexpected strength—an unyielding spirit contained in a mere frame of glass.

"Let's head back," Finn suggested, but Lara shook her head.

"Not yet. I want to capture the sunset."

Grinning, Finn stepped aside, allowing her the space to settle down. She spun her wheelchair to face the horizon, positioning herself for the perfect shot. As the sky ignited in a tapestry of reds, oranges, and violets, Lara was ready to frame her masterpiece.

Pressing the shutter once more, she captured not just an image but a sentiment—unfettered joy and profound freedom encapsulated in a single photograph.

In that moment, Lara understood: each snap was a heartbeat, each frame a testament to her journey. This was only the beginning, and she was eager for all the moments yet to come.

SHADOWS OF DOUBT: FACING THE CHALLENGE

The sun hung low in the sky, casting a warm glow over the stunning landscapes that rolled out before Lara Hargrove. With her camera perched on her lap, she felt both anticipation and a tightening knot of uncertainty in her chest. Today was pivotal, a day to confront her shadows of doubt, and as much as she tried to suppress it, the challenge loomed larger than any breathtaking vista.

"Ready for an adventure?" Finn O'Reilly's voice boomed with infectious enthusiasm as he adjusted the straps of the backpack slung over his shoulder. He was ever the charismatic guide, his passion for exploration palpable. But today, as Lara looked at the rugged trail ahead, the sense of freedom she had felt during previous excursions began to flutter away.

"Just need to frame my thoughts first," Lara murmured, forcing a smile as Evelyn Baxter adjusted her camera settings nearby, glancing over with a knowing look. Evelyn's support had been unwavering, but even her vibrant spirit couldn't fully banish the doubts gnawing at Lara's resolve.

"Let's not just capture the great outdoors today, but also capture what's inside us," Evelyn said, a sparkle of mischief in her eyes. "You've got this, Lara."

As they set off, the path twisted through thickets of wildflowers, where the air was thick with fragrant blooms and the buzzing of industrious bees. Finn led the way, skipping ahead to scout out the best spots, his tales of discovery flowing effortlessly. "Did you know this place used to be a resting spot for ancient travellers?" he shared, glancing back at Lara, who found herself smiling despite her growing fear. However, joy was cramped by her insecurity – would she truly be able to capture the essence of this adventure?

A gentle but powerful reminder echoed in her mind – the delicate balancing act between her passion for photography and the limitations her wheelchair sometimes imposed. Once again, her mind slipped into the darkened corners of her insecurities. What if her pictures didn't translate the thrill she felt when creating them? What if she failed... again?

The sudden appearance of Theo Marquez broke her thoughts, his curious eyes flickering with intensity. "Lara, let's work on pulling more emotion into your shots today. Embrace the challenge," he encouraged, his presence exuding an air of mystery and mastery over his craft. His words held weight, delving deeper into her spirit, igniting a spark of determination she was desperate to hold onto, even as self-doubt lingered.

As Lara reached for her camera, a sudden jolt of determination surged through her, momentarily silencing the doubts that rattled within. "Okay, let's do this," she announced, feeling the vibrations of her voice solidify her intentions.

They trekked up a grassy hillside, with the beauty of nature opening before them like a visual symphony. "See how the light fractures through the trees? That's what makes a photograph come alive!" Finn shouted, his excitement sparking a familiar thrill within her. They settled near a secluded rock that jutted out, providing a perfect view of an expansive valley embracing the horizon.

"Here, Lara," Evelyn directed as she arranged a cluster of wildflowers, "Look through the lens and let it align with your emotions. We're framing more than just nature; we're framing your feelings."

As Lara focused her lens on the blossoms, cloaked in hues of amber and violet, she felt for a fleeting moment that the worries tethering her down might dissipate. She snapped a few shots, relishing the creative freedom that ignited her spirit, feeling every inch of the world through each frame. But among the beauty, shadows still threatened to engulf her spirit, and she couldn't ignore the nagging voice whispering worse-case scenarios in the depths of her mind.

Noticing her pensive silence, Theo stepped closer. "Every artist has their fears, Lara. What you capture does not need to be perfect; it merely needs to reflect your truth," he affirmed, offering a comforting encouragement. "Let's not hide behind those shadows. Embrace them; they're as much a part of your story as the light."

"It's easy to say," Lara whispered, partially defeated but still yearning to shake free from the constraints of her own thoughts. "What if my truth isn't enough?"

Jasper Woodson, the eccentric resident of the nearby village, happened upon them as he often did when the day lured him outdoors. "Ah, there's nothing quite like shadow and light dancing together!" he crowed, plopping down on a nearby boulder. "Every tale, every photograph tells of its own battle – shadows to wrestle against, light to emerge victorious." His twinkling eyes bore insight, his unusual wisdom often illuminating aspects of life that those encircled in their struggles failed to see.

As she thought about his words, a gust of wind swept over the hillside, rustling the wildflower petals and creating a riot of motion beneath the clear sky, awakening her senses. The dance of light and shadow was not just a metaphor for photography but a reminder of her own experiences. She raised her camera and captured the fleeting moment, the contrasting elements reminding her that beauty existed even amidst challenges.

"Let's try something different!" Scarlett Rivers shouted from her perch further along the ridge. She had spotted a heart-stopping view of the valley below, drawing their eyes toward the cliff's edge. "Let's make this adventure a little more daring!"

Despite Lara feeling a pang of trepidation, a flicker of excitement chased it away. "Let's do it," she breathed, a burgeoning sense of audacity igniting within her. The group rallied behind her, offering assurance as they navigated the rocky path toward the heightened terrain.

Once at the edge, Lara was spellbound. The majesty of the landscape unfolded, with hues transforming under the changing light like an artist's palette. She manoeuvred her wheelchair closer, positioning herself where she could capture both the valley and the ethereal lighting that washed over everything.

"Look for unconventional angles," Theo suggested, kneeling down beside her. "Exploration is about seeking surprises." With newfound understanding, she adjusted her lens, capturing the world from her unique perspective. The images produced were not just photographs; they were a powerful narrative of her journey – echoing her struggles, bursting with the promise of adventure.

However, amidst the exhilaration, another wave of doubt crashed over her. What if she didn't convey the essence of this moment in the frames she captured? Just as she was about to give in to those unsettling thoughts once again, Evelyn pulled her closer: "Don't you dare hide from your brilliance, Lara. Let everything about this moment spill onto the canvas of your photographs."

Evelyn's encouragement rang true. With a steady breath, Lara took the leap; hands steady, she clicked the shutter, harnessing the spirit of the place – a mix of courage, beauty, and raw authenticity. Each frame added depth to her journey, reminding her that linear paths weren't truly real, but rather a blend of winding roads. As she reviewed the shots, a wave of warmth washed over her – she had not only framed stunning views but had reflected her own evolution, victories born through the shadows.

"Are we ready to push those limits further?" Finn's voice echoed, pulling her back from her thoughts. "There's a waterfall a few miles ahead, and I know just the spot for creating an epic shot."

Lara chuckled, now fully embracing her journey. She locked eyes with her friends – Theo, Evelyn, Finn, and the others – who stood beside her, support woven seamlessly through their camaraderie. Though shadows of doubt still flickered in the corners, she felt bolstered by their presence.

"Let's go, then," Lara declared, her spirit ignited with newfound confidence. Today was not just about photography; it was about unmasking the beauty hidden in the shadows and embracing every element of her journey without fear.

She rolled forward, her heart filled with anticipation, thrilled by the challenges waiting ahead – and feeling, for the first time, that the shadows of doubt were simply a backdrop, framing the vibrant story she was meant to tell.

A PHOTOGRAPH'S WHISPER: STORIES UNTOLD

The sun dipped low over the horizon, painting the sky in hues of orange and purple, casting a warm glow on the cobbled streets of the quaint village where Lara Hargrove found herself. Every corner seemed to whisper secrets, beckoning her to uncover their untold stories. With her camera nestled firmly in her lap, she felt the familiar flutter of excitement rise within her – the promise of adventure lingered in the air like the sweet scent of blooming jasmine.

"Just look at that light!" Evelyn exclaimed, peering over Lara's shoulder as they rounded a corner. "Now that is going to create a stunning backdrop for your next shot!"

Lara's fingers instinctively gripped the camera, her spirit igniting with the possibilities ahead of them.

"You're right! I can almost see the photograph in my mind," she replied, a grin breaking across her face as she envisioned the scene before her. There was a stillness to the evening that echoed with potential, and as she focused her lens, the world transformed into a canvas of vibrant colours and intricate details.

Finn O'Reilly, her charming local guide, strolled beside them, his eyes shimmering with enthusiasm. "This village isn't just about picturesque views, you know," he interjected. "Each stone has a story, waiting for someone like you to discover it." His voice, low and rich, wrapped around Lara like a comforting embrace, and she felt her heart quicken at the thought of the untold narratives hidden beneath the surface.

"Then let's dig deeper!" Lara declared, an adventurous glint in her eyes, as she scanned the landscape before them. Her courage, compounded by the camaraderie of her friends, allowed her to dream wider. Today, she wouldn't just capture images; she would capture echoes of history through her photographs.

With Evelyn's keen eye for detail and Finn's knack for storytelling, they ventured into the heart of the village, passing centuries-old buildings entwined with climbing vines and flower boxes bursting with colours. Lara's camera clicked rhythmically, fulfilling her purpose as she now wielded it like a magical wand. Each frame was an opportunity to unveil life beyond her wheelchair.

As they paused to admire an ancient stone fountain, the melodic trickle of water seemed to unlock secrets of its past. "This fountain was built long before the village was even a thought," Finn said, gesturing animatedly. "Rumour has it that lovers would whisper their dreams into the water, hoping it would carry their wishes into the world."

"Just imagine the photographs we could create here!" Evelyn exclaimed, her excitement palpable. "Lara, capture a shot of the water reflecting the last rays of sun!"

Lara agreed wholeheartedly; the scene before her was teeming with stories. She carefully adjusted her camera, angling for the perfect light. The fountain stood proud against the backdrop of the setting sun, casting a gentle glow. When she clicked the shutter, it felt like more than just a photograph – it was a moment that encapsulated generations of hopes, dreams, and promises whispered to the winds.

As dusk settled, the village transformed into a playground of shadows and light, and Lara found herself drawn to a quaint little bookshop. The worn wooden door creaked as they entered, revealing shelves crammed full of stories waiting to be read.

There, in the corner, a familiar figure hunched over a collection of dusty tomes.

"Jasper Woodson!" Lara called, her voice laced with delight. The eccentric old man looked up, his wise eyes twinkling with mischief.

"Ah, my dear Lara," he welcomed with warmth, adjusting his spectacles as if readying himself for a grand tale. "What brings you to my nook of narratives?"

"Stories!" she beamed, glancing at her friends. "I want to capture the heart and soul of this village through my photographs. Are there any tales you could share?"

Jasper leaned back in his chair, the aged wood creaking beneath him. "Every place holds legends, my girl. Why, this very bookshop once housed a young girl whose curiosity led her to treasures beyond imagination! But alas, she had to face her fears before finding them." His voice wove a spell as vivid as the richest paintings.

Enthralled by his words, Lara listened intently, her imagination running wild. Each tale sparked inspiration, igniting her drive to seek out the stories hidden within the lens of her camera. She snapped photos of the quaint bookshop interior, determined to capture not just the image, but the essence of curiosity that filled the air.

A PHOTOGRAPH'S WHISPER: STORIES UNTOLD

As they meandered out of the shop, Finn paused under the twinkling fairy lights that adorned the street. "You know, Lara, the best photographs often come from unexpected moments – the unscripted ones that tell a deeper story," he mused.

With that, a burst of inspiration struck Lara. "Let's explore further! There may be stories hiding in plain sight." Together, they traversed alleyways cloaked in shadows, searching for remnants of life that spoke to the essence of their adventure.

Suddenly, Lara caught a glimpse of movement out of the corner of her eye. A street artist sat on a corner, deftly painting the world that surrounded him. The strokes of his brush were quick and confident, and as he stepped back to evaluate his work, mystical colours danced on the canvas.

"Look at the way he captures light!" Evelyn whispered, her eyes wide with admiration. "Can you believe how he replaces the ordinary with the extraordinary?"

Lara nodded in agreement. With a few quick clicks, she captured the artist at work – a moment that encapsulated the raw creative spirit thriving in the heart of the village. It was as if she caught his inspiration in mid-air, radiating like the sun that had just set beyond the horizon.

Despite the fatigue that tugged gently at her limbs, the thrill of the day filled Lara with vitality. Just then, a familiar face approached. Theo Marquez, the enigmatic wildlife photographer she had crossed paths with earlier in her journey, joined them.

"Ah, Lara, I see you've found the magic of storytelling!" he exclaimed, leaning on his camera bag with a love of nature burning in his eyes. "Every photograph you take weaves another thread into the fabric of a broader picture."

"We're trying to discover the stories untold," Lara shared, her eyes sparkling with passion. "The stories that shape communities, inspire change, and remind us of our shared humanity."

Theo nodded knowingly. "Stories are the lifeblood of existence. They remind us of why we're here and connect us to one another. Let me show you something…" He beckoned her to follow, the group trailing closely behind.

They arrived at a park just outside the village, where the last golden rays of sun created a dance through the leaves. Theo guided her to a majestic old tree, its gnarled branches reaching out in ancient wisdom. "This tree has withstood storms and witnessed decades of life," he said softly. "It has stories where you least expect to find them."

A PHOTOGRAPH'S WHISPER: STORIES UNTOLD

Lara knelt close, her camera poised to capture the intricate patterns formed by the bark and the gentle sway of the leaves. She felt a profound connection, a whisper echoing through her heart. Each photograph she took felt heavy with wonder, as though the stories of the tree entwined with her own.

"I can feel it," she murmured, a quiet reverence lacing her voice. "This place breathes life, and every click of the shutter brings it to light."

"And so will you," Theo replied, his gaze steady. "Through your lens, you'll unleash these stories; through your heart, you'll give them the life they deserve."

As the last light of day slipped away, Lara knew this was merely the beginning. Each photograph, a brushstroke of life capturing hope, dreams, and resilience, whispered tales yet to be unveiled. A newfound determination settled in her heart as she looked upon her friends, each a vital thread in this tapestry of adventure.

The world was laden with untold stories, beautiful and profound, waiting patiently for someone unafraid to chase after them. And in that moment, Lara embraced her own freedom – not just through the lens of her camera, but by embracing the kaleidoscope of lives unfolding around her.

THE ALLEY OF INSPIRATION

The narrow alleyway of Willow Lane whispered secrets along its cobblestone path, partially hidden between tall, charming buildings draped in climbing ivy. To the casual observer, it might have seemed a forgotten pocket of the city, but to Lara Hargrove, it was a treasure trove waiting to be unfurled.

Today, she rolled her wheelchair into the alley, her heart beating with anticipation. Orange and gold hues of autumn leaves fluttered on the ground, creating a rugged carpet against the dark stones. It was a tapestry of colour and texture that made her pulse race with eagerness. Evelyn Baxter, with her fiery red hair gleaming like the sun, ambled beside her, camera slung across her shoulder, eyes sparkling with the same adventurous spirit that drove them both.

"Isn't it magical?" Evelyn breathed, a hint of wonder in her voice. She knelt beside Lara, peering at the scattered leaves, ready to explore angles for capturing the scene.

Lara grinned, her fingers grazing the edge of her camera, feeling its weight as if it were an extension of her very soul. "Let's document every angle, Ev! This place is bursting with life."

As she turned her camera lens towards a gnarled tree branch jutting over the wall, Finn O'Reilly appeared, his charming grin illuminating the alley. "Thought I'd find you two here. This alley is a local favourite for artists!"

"Artists?" Lara asked, intrigued. "What do you mean?"

Finn leaned in, his voice laden with excitement. "There are murals around the corner, and we're just at the beginning of the artistic magic. Local painters and street artists come here for inspiration. It's an ever-evolving gallery!" He glanced towards an archway at the end of the alley, silhouetted against the brightness of the exterior world beyond. "Come on, let me show you."

With a quiet thrill coursing through her, Lara followed as best she could. The wheels of her chair rolled smoothly over the textured surface, every sound echoing off the brick walls, and Lara felt like she was navigating through a heartbeat of the city itself.

Suddenly, Finn stopped, gesturing at a blank wall. "This," he announced dramatically, "is called the Wall of Stories."

Evelyn gasped, her eyes sparkling at the sight. Murals of all kinds adorned the brick, from vibrant florals and sweeping landscapes to stunning portraits that seemed to spring to life – a kaleidoscope of artistry that echoed the stories of the city and its people.

"Take your time, Lara," Finn encouraged. "Every mural here has a story. Let it speak to you."

As Lara focused her camera at a vivid mural depicting wildflowers in full bloom, she felt an electric surge beneath her skin. Every shot she took felt like capturing magic, a moment of inspiration that breathed life into her very being, a testament to the ability to see and appreciate beauty from different perspectives.

"Did you see the way the petals blend into the sky?" Evelyn raved, hopping up and down with enthusiasm. "It's like the artist wanted to reach for the heavens! You need to capture that!"

"Exactly," agreed Lara with renewed fervour, her fingers dancing over the camera buttons. The lens adjusted, framing the stunning mix of colours

THE ALLEY OF INSPIRATION

that shot up from the base of the mural to the cloud-filled sky. "This is what freedom looks like for me. These stories want to be told."

Just then, Theo Marquez entered the alley, his presence commanding yet serene. His camera hung around his neck, and he approached with a quiet confidence—an unspoken understanding in his eyes.

"Ah, the Wall of Stories," he said, nodding appreciatively. "You're right to be inspired, Lara. Each shade, each brush stroke is a memory captured by the artist. What story are you hoping to tell?"

Lara considered Theo's question, suddenly aware of the responsibility that came with their craft. "I want to show people there's beauty everywhere. Even in places that seem ordinary. This alley... it may seem forgotten, but look at it! It's alive!"

A warm smile crossed Theo's face. "You're exactly right. Embrace that feeling; let it guide your lens." He then motioned toward a particularly striking mural of a lion. "Do you remember when we talked about the primal connection we have with nature? This wall is just like that. It depicts raw emotion through art."

As Lara focused her camera, snapping shot after shot, she felt empowered by the vibrant atmosphere, a sense of purpose coursing through her veins. In the midst of her excitement, modern graffiti met ancient styles, illustrating the melding of time through each spray of paint.

Evelyn emerged from behind the tower of bricks, her own camera poised. "I think I see a story blooming here, Lara! We should showcase our contrasting styles—the spontaneous chaos of urban art paired with your instinctual nature photography."

Lara laughed, a sound bright and full of mirth. "You always know how to frame a moment beautifully, Ev."

They explored deeper into the alley, each nook and cranny revealing more hidden masterpieces. A faded portrait of a woman with soulful eyes caught Lara's attention, the expression striking something profound within her.

"Who do you think she was?" Lara mused, adjusting her focus to a shallow depth of field to capture the emotion in the mural.

Finn paused beside her, eyes narrowing as he observed the artwork. "She's the double-edged sword of inspiration—strong yet vulnerable. The artist wanted to remind us that everyone has a story worth telling."

With a newfound perspective, Lara leaned closer, intent on preserving the soul of the mural through her lens, every inch of paint now bursting with stories only she could unveil. Her heart raced as she recorded the fleeting moment, a tangible dream captured against the textured canvas of life.

Suddenly, Scarlett Rivers came rushing into the alley, her boundless energy demanding attention. "You guys! You won't believe what I found nearby! Are we ready for adventure?"

Lara's heart skipped. "What did you discover?"

Scarlett grinned, revealing it all like an artist unveiling their latest masterpiece. "An abandoned factory! Perfect for some urban exploration–imagine the angles, the rawness. You can document the layers of history, how nature slowly reclaims it!"

"If you think that's a good idea, count me in!" Lara enthused, her mind racing. "It's time to blend urban decay with the beauty of nature. Can you imagine the stories hidden within those walls?"

Evelyn nodded, tempted by the thrill. "There's something alluring about unravelling the forgotten, especially with our cameras in hand."

As they prepared to roll out, Lara turned her gaze back to the Wall of Stories, inhaling the scents of paint and history entwined. She felt invigorated, the alley whispering promises of exploration.

Just as they were about to leave, a scruffy old man appeared–a figure that seemed lifted straight from time. "You lot love this alley, eh?" he asked with a sly smile, leaning on a wall adorned with bold quotes and vibrant characters. "I've been coming here for years; the stories here feed my soul."

Jasper Woodson was an eclectic presence, forever a part of the alley's charm. He spun yarns of yesteryear wrapped in the flavour of experiences he savoured. "It's not just about what you capture, but also about what you feel. The true art lies in the heart of the beholder."

Lara nodded thoughtfully, excitement coursing through her once more at the prospect of endless narratives waiting to unfold. The alley was a reflection of her journey—each mural a piece of this vibrant city that defied limitations and embraced freedom.

With her camera cradled in her hands, Lara knew that she'd found her heartbeat amidst the murals, letters, and tales woven into the alley. It was here that her spirit soared, buoyed by inspiration.

"Let's go," she declared, her wheels rolling forward, guided by a luminous path of creativity and adventure that awaited just beyond the alley's exit.

And thus, through the lens, she would continue her journey, capturing the untamed beauty of the world that called to her heart.

BREAKING THE FRAME: A NEW PERSPECTIVE

As dawn broke over the hills, golden rays spilled across the landscape, lighting the path to new adventures. Lara Hargrove adjusted her camera, its strap snug against her shoulder, and took a moment to breathe in the crisp morning air. Today was going to be different; today, she would break free from the frame she had long accepted.

Finn O'Reilly stood beside her, his bright smile radiating an infectious enthusiasm that matched the sun above. "Are you ready, Lara?" he asked, glancing at the rugged trail leading into the emerald forest. His eyes sparkled with an adventurous fire that ignited Lara's spirit.

"Ready as I'll ever be!" she replied, her voice tinged with excitement. Today was not just about taking photographs; it was about reshaping her whole world-view. With Finn by her side, she felt empowered to explore the unknown.

Their journey began with a gentle roll down a cobblestone path that twisted through the quaint village. The colourful homes, each adorned with vibrant blooms, beckoned her camera. Lara positioned the lens to capture the picturesque scene, but Evelyn's voice echoed in her mind, reminding her of the importance of framing a shot. "Focus on the details, Lara. The magic isn't just in the grand vistas, but in the small stories too."

With a flick of the shutter, the moment was frozen in time—a lively home filled with laughter, the sun's golden light filtering through floral arches. She could feel the magic radiate from her photographs even before they captured the vibrancy of the scene.

As they embarked deeper into the woods, Finn led her towards a hidden waterfall. The sound of rushing water grew louder, invigorating Lara's senses. "Wait until you see this!" Finn exclaimed, excitement spilling from his words.

As they reached the clearing, Lara was struck by the sight before her. Sunlight showered the cascading water, creating a prism of colours that danced in the air. "This is... incredible!" she breathed, her camera quivering in her hands with anticipation.

She framed the shot, allowing her imagination to run wild. Each droplet of water seemed to hold a story, each ray of sunlight a memory waiting to be uncovered. Just as she was about to snap the photograph, Theo Marquez emerged from behind a tree, his camera poised.

"You're capturing the spirit of this place," he said, his deep voice full of warmth. Lara had admired Theo from afar–his work in wildlife photography had that unique flair that made the heart race. "But," he added, tilting his head toward the falls, "try capturing it differently."

Lara furrowed her brows. "Differently? How?"

"Instead of focusing on the waterfall itself, look for reflections in the water, or the textures of the rocks beneath," he explained, gesturing to the surface where light shimmered. "Every frame can tell countless stories; it's up to you to find them."

Inspired by Theo's words, Lara repositioned her angle. As the lens caught the glimmer of the sun through the rippling water, it revealed a world beyond the ordinary. An intricate tapestry of light and shadow unveiled itself. She let out a joyful laugh as she pressed the shutter, her heartbeat syncing with the thrum of adventure coursing through her.

Their joyful euphoria continued, but as they ventured deeper, the path grew steeper. Lara's wheelchair bumped across roots and became a familiar challenge. Finn noticed her strain and paused, concern evident on his face. "Do you want to take a break?"

Lara's spirit remained unbroken. "No way! This is part of the adventure, remember?" She remembered Evelyn urging her to embrace every challenge, each struggle a chance for growth, even the fear that shrouded her at times.

She breathed in and fortified herself, pushing forward with renewed determination. As they neared the top, they were greeted by an expansive view over the valley below. It was as though they stood on the brink of the world, the horizon stretching endlessly.

Lara positioned her camera for a sweeping panorama, yet as she peered through the viewfinder, she felt something within her shift. The vastness of the landscape suggested an invitation, a call to embrace the freedom that lay beyond her physical constraints. Her heart raced with the thought of capturing this essence—not just as a photograph but as a feeling she could eternalise.

The click of the shutter resonated with a confident finality. She marvelled at the image, each element perfectly aligned: the rolling hills, the vibrant sky, and the little patch of wildflowers just below, stubbornly thriving against all odds.

"This is so much more than just a photo, isn't it?" Finn mused, even as a hint of wind scattered leaves around them.

"It is," Lara replied, her voice steady. "I'm starting to see how all these frames tell not just one story, but many."

Suddenly, from behind a nearby rock, Scarlett Rivers emerged, a whirlwind of energy in her neon gear. "Did someone say adventure?" she chimed, eyes sparkling. "There's nothing better than the thrill of adrenaline and the beauty of nature combined! Come on, follow me. I know a place where we can get the shot of a lifetime."

Lara's heart raced at the prospect of new challenges. "What are we doing?" she asked, intrigued.

"Rock climbing! Nothing too intense, but just enough to get your pulse racing and a fresh perspective on capturing that beauty," Scarlett replied with infectious enthusiasm.

With Finn and Theo beside her, Lara welcomed the challenge. Each ascent revealed new vistas—a rich moody sky, sharp rocks bursting with wildflowers, and even glimpses of elusive wildlife.

She adapted with every push and pull, easing her way towards the summit, determination propelling her wheel forward.

At the top, Lara felt breathless—not just from the climb but from the realisation that her perspective had shifted. She placed her hands on the very edge of the cliff, the world sprawled magnificently below her.

"Now, this..." she snapped photographs, understanding that she was capturing this moment not just for herself, but for others who might feel confined by their limitations. Each frame spoke of hope, resilience, and the beauty of overcoming.

"Some would say this is an unusual way of connecting with nature," Theo remarked, eyeing her frame. "But what you're doing is revolutionary. You're breaking the frame, and it's about time."

Later, as the sun began to set, they found themselves gathered around a fire, sharing stories and laughing heartily. Evelyn's jokes made everyone chuckle, her wit illuminating the space like the flames that danced before them. Conversations flowed, merging the extraordinary tales with their beloved photographs, filling the air with dreams and aspirations.

Nadia, ever the mentor, brought forth a discussion about the stories behind each shot.

"It's one thing to capture the image, but another to convey its heart," she explained. "What we see through the lens is only half the tale; the other half is your voice."

Lara felt invigorated by her words. As they delved into their shared experiences, she recognised the importance of intertwining her adventure with others' narratives, capturing not just images but voices longing to be heard.

"Every photograph holds a piece of your spirit," Nadia continued, "when you share it, others can find connections too."

The word lingered in Lara's mind: connections. With each photograph she took, she would not only frame moments but also weave together paths of understanding, bridging lives through the beauty of her lens.

As she drifted off to sleep, Lara's spirit soared. The day had freed her in a way she'd never imagined. Tomorrow would bring new discoveries, new adventures, and further opportunities to embrace her freedom through the art of photography.

Tonight, she had not just broken the frame; she had transcended it entirely. And with that, Lara's journey had truly just begun.

JOURNEY TO THE EDGE: NATURE'S CANVAS

The sun hung low in the sky, casting a golden hue across the rugged cliffs and sweeping valleys of their latest destination. Lara Hargrove sat in her wheelchair, her camera poised and ready, eyes glinting with anticipation. This was more than just another outing; it was a promise of adventure and discovery, a canvas awaiting the touch of her lens.

"Are you ready for this, Lara?" Finn O'Reilly's voice broke through her reverie, infused with a playful challenge. With his charming smile and infectious enthusiasm, he had a way of making even the most daunting paths seem inviting.

"Aren't we supposed to edge our way to the cliffs?" she replied, feigning nonchalance, her heart racing with excitement. Lara had learned to embrace the thrill of chasing beauty through her lens, and this journey, into the heart of the wilderness, was a chance to capture nature in all its magnificent forms.

"Absolutely! But you know, the journey to the edge is half the fun," he winked, gesturing for Evelyn Baxter, her witty best friend who was already scouting the area for the best compositions.

Together, they wheeled towards the towering cliffs, greenery spilling over the rocky edges like a vibrant cloak. Lara felt the wind wrap around her, a whispering reminder that the world outside her usual confines was alive and breathing.

"Lara, this angle is much better!" Evelyn exclaimed, waving her hand towards an old, gnarled tree that clung to the cliff's edge. "The contrast between its resilience and the vast sky behind it will be stunning."

"Okay, let's frame it," Lara replied, adjusting the settings on her camera. The tree stood defiantly against the whims of nature, reflecting her own journey. Unlike Lara's previous apprehensions, she now recognised her limitations as merely invitations for innovation. Click—each shot was a powerful narrative unfolding through her lens.

As they set up, Theo Marquez appeared, his presence quiet yet compelling. "You're capturing nature's stories, Lara," he said, leaning slightly closer to inspect her work. "But remember, sometimes the best images are found in the moments we least expect."

Lara exchanged a glance with Finn, whose smile widened—he relished Theo's unpredictable wisdom. Together, they were a troupe in this wild theatre, filled with anticipation for what lay ahead. With every shot, Lara felt herself connecting deeper with her surroundings, as if the earth itself spoke to her, merging her spirit with its magnificent expanse.

The trio explored hidden trails that led to stunning overlooks, where the valleys sprawled below them like an emerald tapestry. "This place is like a natural gallery, showcasing Mother Nature's finest art," Finn mused, spreading his arms wide. "You just wait until you see it at sunset."

Suddenly, the air shifted as clouds began to gather ominously in the distance. "Looks like we might have a storm coming," Evelyn noted, frowning slightly. The rugged beauty of nature, she recognised, was not without its unpredictability. But adventure was entwined with such dangers, and Lara felt a surge of adrenaline at the thought.

"What if we go further?" Scarlett Rivers' bold spirit, always daring and relentless, floated through Lara's mind. Inspired by the enthusiastic extreme sports enthusiast, Lara felt her resolve strengthen. "Let's chase the storm."

"Chase the storm? With a camera?" Evelyn laughed, her eyes glimmering with the spirit of adventure. "That's both exhilarating and reckless!"

But Lara's heart soared at the thought. She knew it was the edge that made her feel truly alive. With encouragement from Finn, she steered her wheelchair into the deeper recesses of the landscape, heart hammering with the thrill of uncertainty.

As the wind picked up, carrying the scent of impending rain, they spotted an arching view over the valleys. "This is it!" Finn declared, positioning himself beside her as she set up her camera.

"Hold that pose!" Lara exclaimed playfully, snapping a quick photo.

Their laughter echoed against the cliffs, a jubilant sound swallowed by the unyielding wilderness. Above, grey clouds bustled, and a crack of thunder rolled ominously. It held a strange allure—a reminder of nature's raw power.

Encircled by the beauty of the moment, Lara whispered, "Can you imagine if we could capture the storm rolling in?" The idea fired her imagination, revealing a vivid narrative aching to emerge.

"Let's do it!" Finn encouraged, his voice carrying an infectious enthusiasm.

Theo grinned, supportive yet serious, "A storm offers a unique opportunity. You must embrace chaos to find real beauty."

Just then Emilio Cruz appeared, his custom camera rig in hand, his face bright with enthusiasm. "I thought I'd find you all here. I've made a few adjustments for those dramatic shots," he said, as if conjuring new possibilities with every word spoken.

"Emilio, we're about to shoot the storm!" Lara exclaimed, her heart racing, "Can you help me with this rig?"

Together, they affixed the revolutionary contraption to her camera, enabling her to capture angles she'd never thought possible. It provided her the freedom to seize the tempest from new heights. The anticipation bubbled like a fizzy drink, igniting Lara's spirit.

As the first drops of rain began to patter around them, Lara wheeled forward, feeling every ounce of exhilaration coursing through her. The landscape transformed strangely in the grey light. With every shutter click, the sky was alive. Framed through the lens, the clouds swirled in a dramatic dance—nature was showcasing its tempestuous soul.

"Lara, look at that!" Evelyn called, pointing towards a radiant double rainbow forming across the horizon. The juxtaposition of chaos and beauty struck her, and she turned to catch that fleeting moment as it stretched across the sky, all reflected through her camera's viewfinder.

"Got it!" Lara exclaimed, snapping several shots in quick succession, her heart swelling with triumph. Each click was a piece of her liberation, a declaration that the world, with its infinite wonders, was hers to capture and cherish.

Nadia Thompson, who had been observing them from a distance, approached, her eyes glistening with admiration. "You're weaving a stunning story, Lara. The union of the storm and the rainbow is a poignant reminder that beauty often arises from chaos."

With unexpected support from Jasper Woodson, who had appeared alongside them, weaving tales of ancient storms that shaped the landscape, Lara felt deeply rooted in the tapestry of life surrounding her.

"Legends breath life into these moments," he remarked, his voice rich with history. "Capture that energy; let it ripple through your work."

With renewed purpose, Lara turned her camera skyward, weaving between the contrasting hues of grey tempest and vibrant arcs of colour, creating a narrative that spoke beyond her own limitations. Each photo was a brushstroke on the canvas of her adventure.

In the distance, the pitter-patter of rain transformed into a steady downpour. The world around her blurred, revealing a dreamscape painted in vibrant watercolours. As she wheeled closer to the edge, she felt a sense of communion with nature, a powerful connection binding her to the very core of existence.

"Lara!" Finn shouted, excitement bubbling in his voice. "Look at those clouds! Let's chase the light!"

With a roar of laughter and determination, they raced along the rugged terrain, the storm behind them transforming the landscape into an otherworldly realm that begged to be captured. As they approached the edge of the cliff, Lara felt an invigorating mix of joy and fright—the thrill of life in its purest form.

"Today, we're not just photographers; we are explorers!" Evelyn exclaimed, eyes sparkling with adrenaline.

And in that moment, Lara knew her journey had spiralled into something transformative, infused with the essence of freedom that had been bottled up inside her for far too long. She was on the cutting edge, capturing the transient beauty of nature's tempestuous embrace.

As the storm raged on and the rain drummed upon her skin, she smiled, exhilarated and free. This was more than just photography; it was her testament to resilience—a vibrant narrative framed by nature itself.

THE MAGIC OF LIGHT: DANCING WITH SHADOWS

The morning sun spilled through the open window, splashing warm hues across Lara's bedroom like a painter shaking an exuberant palette. Today was no ordinary day; it was a day of promise, a day to embrace the magic that lay in every corner of the world beyond her window. The air filled with the scent of fresh coffee, and the murmurs of Evelyn, her best friend, wafted in from the kitchen as she prepared their breakfast.

"Lara! Are you ready to catch some shadows today?" Evelyn's voice rang out with a blend of excitement and mischief.

"Ready as I'll ever be! I have a feeling today is going to be incredible," Lara replied, spinning her wheelchair towards the sunlit scene. The anticipation ignited in her chest, reminding her that while the world had its challenges, it was filled with moments waiting to be captured.

After breakfast, Evelyn helped Lara load her modified camera rig–thanks to the ingenious Emilio Cruz–into her lap. The new attachment enabled Lara to explore angles that were previously out of reach. With every click, she had the power to reshape the narrative of her own life. They were meeting Finn O'Reilly today, the charming local guide who had swiftly become a friend. He had an uncanny ability to uncover hidden treasures, illuminating overlooked details that made each moment sparkle.

The trio convened at the edge of a sun-dappled park, where the elegant silhouettes of trees swayed gently in the wind. Finn's eyes lit up as he gestured towards a serene pond cradled by willows. "Look at the way the light dances on the water! This place is perfect for what I have in mind–you'll see real magic today."

Lara's heart raced with anticipation. As they approached the pond, the sun peeked between the leaves, casting intricate patterns that flickered across the water's surface, as if nature were performing a delicate ballet of light and shadow.

"Let's capture those reflections," Finn suggested, his enthusiasm infectious. Lara swung her camera into action, positioning it to focus on the glints of sunlight dancing on the ripples.

"What do you see?" Evelyn asked, peering over Lara's shoulder.

"The water is like a canvas," Lara mused, adjusting the lens to zero in on a patch where the sunlight sparkled—a thousand tiny stars igniting at once. "It tells a story of light meeting darkness, reflecting beauty in the simplest forms. Each ripple is a journey."

The synchronous sound of a shutter clicking echoed as Lara captured the scene. With each shot, she felt the essence of freedom flow through her—a talent she had always possessed but was only beginning to understand.

"Let's try something different," Finn suggested, pulling out his own camera. "Let's catch those shadows that dance beneath the trees." With a determined twinkle in his eye, he marched towards a cluster of tall, old oaks.

Following him, Lara felt a new urgency. By framing darkness with the light, they could capture more than just the visual—they could incorporate emotion, the essence of a moment. A fleeting dance that thrived in contrast.

"Stand there!" Finn pointed to a vibrant patch of sunlight streaming between branches and dappled shadows.

Lara moved effortlessly, aimed her camera, and took a shot that told a story of entangled lives—her own permanent shadows intertwined with those of her companions.

"Let me show you how it's done," Finn said, demonstrating how to play with the light and shadows by positioning himself under the trees, creating shapes and expressions that seemed to breathe. He was a master at bringing forth the unspoken narratives lurking in the smudged corners of their surroundings.

Silhouetted against the backdrop of light, he struck a pose worthy of an artist. Lara captured the moment—a dance of artistry, light, and shadows that ignited a desire within her to keep exploring.

Suddenly, the air thickened with intrigue as an unexpected figure emerged from behind the trees: Theo Marquez. The mysterious wildlife photographer had an ethereal quality about him that intrigued Lara.

"Mind if I join you?" The soft timbre of Theo's voice pulled them all into his orbit. "I couldn't help but overhear your aim to capture shadows."

"Absolutely!" Lara enthused, a rush of excitement coursing through her. The gathering of artists provided an electric atmosphere, filled with creative camaraderie.

THE MAGIC OF LIGHT: DANCING WITH SHADOWS

"Here's a trick," Theo said, adjusting his camera. "Shadows can reveal truths that the light sometimes hides." He demonstrated as he stepped into the shadows, his physical form almost blending with the trees, illustrating that even darkness has its own narrative.

Entranced, Lara watched as Theo's lens captured the essence of the moment. It wasn't about the absence of light; it was about the stories that shadows whispered. She began to see her own reflections within those shadows—the struggles, the stories untold—unfolding with each click.

"Why don't we find some bold contrasts?" Evelyn suggested, her artistic flair sparkling in her eyes. "I remember a spot in the village where we can explore the play between light and shadow even more!"

With renewed energy, they set off for the village square. The sun dipped lower in the sky, drenching the cobblestones in a golden hue while casting elongated shadows that danced among the arches and doorways.

"Look at that!" Lara exclaimed, pointing her camera towards an old lamppost, its silhouette sharp against the fading light. The play of shadow against the ancient brick wall framed a story of time long past, one that silently echoed with history.

"Perfect! Let's explore a bit further," Finn encouraged, igniting Lara's adventurous spirit.

As they roamed, each turn revealed a tapestry of contrasts–blooming flowers defiant against the cool shadows of the afternoon, the sunlight catching in brimming puddles from recent rains, and residents going about their day, unknowingly part of the artistic narrative Lara was weaving through her photos.

"Every shadow," Theo explained, "is a reminder that light persists. Even in the dark, there is beauty waiting to be seen." His words resonated deeply with Lara, prompting her to explore the layers of light and shadow in her own life.

With an exuberant burst of laughter, Scarlett Rivers, the daredevil extreme sports enthusiast, rode into the square. "What are you all doing? Come on! There's more to capture!" Her fiery spirit contrasted with the tranquillity they had embraced, yet it intrigued Lara.

"You're right! Let's find some excitement!" Evelyn replied, her enthusiasm matching Scarlett's.

They ventured towards the park's edge, where soft hills cascaded into low valleys, perfect for an impromptu photo shoot filled with motion. Lara's heart thrummed with the thrill of spontaneity.

THE MAGIC OF LIGHT: DANCING WITH SHADOWS

Scarlett flashed a grin and raced alongside the ridge, her silhouette painting dynamic strokes against the fading skyline. How fast can she move? Lara aimed her camera, capturing the contrast between the speed of Scarlett and the stillness of the surrounding landscape.

"You see?" Finn clapped Lara's shoulder. "This is what it means to dance with shadows. Using light to expose the excitement and vitality around us."

With each frame, Lara discovered the stories that blossomed in the interplay of light and shadows. Each click documented more than just a moment; they told the tale of a girl before the lens—from the constraints of her wheelchair to the freedom her camera gave her.

By sundown, Lara felt alive, her adventurous spirit only growing stronger. Her camera brimmed with images that now danced in her mind, a tapestry woven not just from sunlight but from unexpected encounters, shadows of doubt turned whispers of joy, and laughter echoing in the golden glow of evening.

As they settled on a bench overlooking the tranquil pond, Lara turned to her friends with gratitude swelling in her heart. "Today was magical. I didn't just capture images; I embraced the stories behind them—the light in every shadow."

Her friends nodded, sharing in the unspoken understanding–that through the lens, they were all intertwined, forever a part of each other's narratives.

With the sunset painting the sky in soft pastels, Lara knew this was just the beginning of her journey–a dance with shadows that ignited a quest for freedom framed through her unique lens.

AN UNEXPECTED COMPANION: FRIENDSHIP UNFOLDS

The morning sun rose lazily over the rolling hills, casting golden rays through the blinds of Lara's modest hotel room. She could hardly contain her excitement, her camera resting in her lap like a patient companion, waiting for their next adventure. Today promised to be different, and she felt it in her bones. With Evelyn busy arranging their breakfast, Lara had one goal in mind—she needed to find a new perspective to frame her growing gallery of life.

"Finn said he knows a really hidden spot," Evelyn chimed in, her curly hair bouncing as she set a tray laden with croissants and fresh fruit on the table. "Something about an old railway bridge overlooking the valley. Sounds like a perfect backdrop!"

"Old railway bridge?" Lara repeated, her heart racing at the thought. "I can almost picture it." As she imagined the scenes, the vibrant hues of nature began to intertwine in her mind, begging to be captured.

After breakfast, the two friends set out to meet Finn, eager but unsure of the day's unfolding landscape. As they rolled along the cobblestone streets, Lara often paused, lifting her camera to snap candid photos of the locals. Each frame she composed revealed a story—a child chasing bubbles, a street musician lost in his melody, a bouquet of flowers spilling vibrancy into the grey stones.

When they arrived at the foot of the hill leading to the bridge, Lara's pulse quickened. The path was steep, covered in rich green moss and scattered leaves. "Are you ready?" asked Evelyn, glancing back at her with mischievous enthusiasm.

"Always," Lara replied, determination sparking in her eyes.

It was just after noon when they reached Finn, who stood waiting at the crest of the hill, an easy smile lighting up his face. "I see the dynamic duo has arrived! Ready to be amazed?"

"Lead the way!" Lara exclaimed, the thrill of exploration igniting in her spirit as the three adventurers moved together, as fluid as the stream gurgling below.

As they navigated through thickets of wildflowers and ancient trees, Finn shared fascinating folklore about the region. His voice wove a tapestry of stories that danced in Lara's mind, causing her to capture unposed moments–the laughter shared between her and Evelyn, the gentle sway of branches above bathed in dappled sunlight, and the way Finn's eyes twinkled with joy.

They finally reached the old railway bridge, a testament to an era long past, festooned in vibrant vines that clung to it like memories refusing to fade. The vast valley spread out below, a riot of colours beneath a cloudless sky–Lara felt as if she had stepped into an artist's canvas.

"Welcome to my favourite spot," Finn declared, gesturing dramatically as if revealing a hidden treasure.

"Amazing…" Lara breathed, her camera falling instinctively into position, clicking the shutter in rapid succession as she absorbed the striking scenery.

Evelyn grabbed Lara's arm, her voice bubbling with excitement. "Look over there! Can you see that cluster of wildflowers just beside the tracks? You must capture that!"

For Lara, each image she snapped felt like a piece of herself surrendered to the landscape. The photographs unravelled frames of pure emotion, colours mixing and vibrating with energy, weaving a story that spoke of resilience and wonder.

But amidst the creative fervour, something unusual caught Lara's eye—a wild fox creeping up towards the bridge's edge. Time slowed as she adjusted her focus, heart pounding in her chest. "Stay still," she whispered, coaxing the moment with her lens. The fox paused, striking an unintentional pose, and with a decisive click, she immortalised its fiery amber coat against the backdrop of verdant green.

"Brilliant shot!" Finn exclaimed, clapping his hands together. Just then, a deep voice broke through the forest tranquillity.

"Do you mind if I join for a moment?"

Lara turned to see a tall figure emerging from the shadows—a mysterious man with tousled hair and intense, observant eyes. The camera slung over his shoulder and the worn leather satchel that hung at his side hinted at a kindred spirit.

"Um, sure! I'm Lara," she offered, as her heart began to dance with excitement over this unexpected ally.

"Theo," he introduced smoothly, stepping closer. "I couldn't help but overhear your enthusiasm. Not often do I see photographers in this remote part."

"What do you photograph?" Evelyn asked, her curiosity piqued.

"Nature mostly, but there's always room for unexpected beauty," Theo replied, glancing over at Lara's camera. "Your frame could tell a fascinating story."

"I try," Lara said, a bit shy but emboldened by their warm welcome. "Today is about capturing freedom. Every click I take feels like another piece of my journey."

"Freedom is a beautiful subject," Theo mused, his gaze lingering thoughtfully over the valley. "But remember, sometimes the moments lie just beyond the frame."

Before Lara could respond, Theo knelt to the ground, gesturing for her to follow. "Get low," he instructed, "and you'll see the ferns from a new angle."

Lara nodded, heart racing with anticipation, as she adjusted her position. The world tilted strangely, now framed by the foliage, seminal and alive. She snapped a picture, her newfound friendship with the wild invoking an unfamiliar but thrilling sense of camaraderie.

Evelyn traded excited glances with Finn, clearly captivated by Theo's infectious passion. The four of them were soon captured in the delight of exploration, weaving around the bridge, unveiling the hidden narratives lurking in every shadow and glimmer of sunlight.

"Do you trust me?" Theo asked, addressing Lara again, intensity glowing in his eyes. With a nod, she braced herself as he moved closer to the edge of the bridge, inviting her to follow. "Sometimes, the best stories are found where you least expect them. Just stay steady, and keep your lens focused."

The adrenaline buzzed through her, the ground dropping away behind her, but it was fuelled by a newfound bond with both Theo and the world. The connection they shared was unfurling, becoming a symphony composed of laughter, shared trials, and trust. Beyond jealousy or fear, they were stitching threads of friendship–a shared story.

As Lara steadied her camera and peered through the viewfinder, Theo drew her attention to a pair of birds hovering nearby. "Capture that expression–feel the moment."

With that encouragement, Lara followed her instinct. The perches were bold against the sky, unfurling their wings and gliding gracefully. They danced on the currents of wind, and she captured them in motion—a photograph brimming with liberation.

"I wish you could see this," Finn whispered, watching the tableau unfold. "You're capturing essence—something we often overlook."

"Essence," Lara echoed softly, the word wrapping around her heart, igniting memories of pain and triumph that shaped her journey. In this moment, the collection of images she was building transcended mere representations; they were affirmations of friendship, courage, and the freedom to embrace life fully.

At last, they all settled on the bridge, under the expansive skyline. Slumped over their cameras, they shared stories of their lives and dreams, laughter echoing through the valley. Lara felt alive in a way, her camera becoming a conduit through which her spirit pulsated: capturing not only the world around her but also the warmth of kindred souls building ties of resilience.

"Sometimes," Theo mused as they basked in the afterglow of adventure, "all it takes to find freedom is an unexpected companion."

Lara looked at her friends, her heart swelling with gratitude. She had ridden the currents of a day filled with stories and had found something deeper—true companionship. Within moments like these, captured forever in her heart, Lara realised that freedom wasn't merely a photograph, but in sharing these experiences with those who understood her journey.

As they prepared to leave, Lara promised herself that this was just the beginning—a series of frames awaiting their story. She smiled, her camera alive with the colours of their friendship, ready to tell of adventure and freedom yet to come.

REFLECTIONS ON THE ROAD: LESSONS FROM THE LENS

The sun hung low in the sky, casting a warm golden hue across the dirt path that wound its way through the lush, sprawling landscape. With each turn of the road, Lara Hargrove felt the exhilarating buzz of possibility coursing through her. The world stretched before her, rich with potential to create stories that would last forever, all waiting to be captured through the lens of her camera.

Finn O'Reilly–always ahead, with his keen eye for adventure–paused to glance back at her, a cheeky grin lighting up his face. "You'd think the road ends here, but trust me, it's just the beginning." His words echoed in her heart, reminding her that sometimes, the most scenic routes lay just around the bend.

As they rolled down the path, Lara lifted her camera, eager to frame a moment. The afternoon light danced through the leaves, casting intricate patterns on the ground. She pressed the shutter, capturing a kaleidoscope of shadows and sunlight, but it was the promise of what lay ahead that left her breathless. With every click, she connected deeper with herself and the vibrant tapestry of life present in every frame.

"Look at that!" Evelyn Baxter exclaimed, perched on a nearby rock, her artistic eye sparkling with energy. She pointed towards a field of wildflowers, each petal clinging desperately to the breeze. "It's like nature is calling you to tell its story!"

Lara laughed and turned her camera towards the riot of colours, feeling a profound sense of gratitude for her friend. Evelyn's support was a constant reminder that every moment captured was not just an image—it was a thread weaving them all together.

As they approached a clearing, a faint rustling caught Lara's attention. She froze, excitement fluttering in her chest. Theo Marquez, the enigmatic wildlife photographer who had joined them a few days prior, seemed at one with the environment, his camera poised and ready. Lara admired the way he moved, blending seamlessly into the wilderness, observing creatures of the wild that others might overlook.

"Patience, Lara," Theo whispered without looking at her. "The magic often lies in the silence."

She took a breath, willing herself to be present in that moment. After a while, a family of deer appeared, gracefully stepping into the sunlight, their sleek bodies glistening as they moved. Lara's heart raced as she positioned her camera, fingers trembling with anticipation. The click of the shutter felt like a heartbeat—a pulsing connection between her and the creatures strikingly beautiful in their vulnerability.

"Got it!" she exclaimed, looking up to see Theo smile, his eyes shining with approval. The shared silence spoke volumes; she had received the lesson of stillness—enough to allow life to unfold in front of her, a discovery whispered only through patience and observation.

With newfound confidence, Lara rolled forward, each push of her wheels infused with the joy of capturing life's fleeting beauty. They ventured into a quaint village where Jasper Woodson, the eccentric old man they had met, beckoned them warmly.

"Tell me, what did you find on the road?" Jasper's voice was rich with intrigue.

Lara shared the story of the deer, and Jasper's weathered face lit up with delight. "Ah, my dear, nature is a teacher. Are you listening to its wisdom?"

Flashes of second thoughts danced in her mind–did she truly understand the world around her? Before she could ponder further, Scarlett Rivers, the fearless extreme sports enthusiast, bounded into view, muttering encouragement to herself under her breath as she prepared for her next venture.

"Lara, you don't want to get left behind!" she called, her excitement infectious. "Let's chase the thrill–I've found a perfect spot for some breathtaking shots along the coast!"

Before Lara could voice a hesitance, she found herself swept up in the whirlwind of energy that was Scarlett. With Finn pushing her chair alongside, they made their way down rugged paths which led to towering cliffs overlooking crashing waves. The adrenaline coursed through her veins, intertwining with the peaceful thrill of nature surrounding her.

As they reached the edge, Lara opened her camera, the wind tugging at her hair. Capturing the ocean's ferocious beauty, she became centred, thriving on the freedom that unfurled in front of her. She was not merely an observer; she was part of a world that embraced her fully, buoyed by the camaraderie between friends.

"Look at that view!" Evelyn exclaimed, snapping photos enthusiastically. The rays of the setting sun filtered through the clouds, igniting the horizon in hues of orange and pink, filling each frame with the promise of tomorrow.

Inspired, Lara's consciousness shifted. She was learning to serenade the world with her camera rather than just observe it. And so a unique teaching was brewing within her; these experiences were not just to be documented, but to live and breathe, resonating in every photograph.

Under the vanishing light, the arrival of Emilio Cruz enriched the moment. A tech-savvy inventor, he was always dreaming up ingenious ways to improve photography. He rolled out a custom rig designed specifically for Lara, his eyes gleaming with pride.

"Now, you can capture everything from angles you've never imagined!" he announced, fitting it to her wheelchair. "Let's take it for a spin!"

Lara stared, awe-struck, as he guided her to set it up. With a flick of a button, her camera transformed, offering new perspectives that sparked her imagination. She was no longer limited; she could shoot from below and above, soaring beyond the lines traditionally drawn.

"Let's do it!" she shouted, feeling an intoxicating blend of excitement. They ventured back to the cliffs where the golden hour bathed everything in ethereal light, and Lara set off, capturing the world anew.

From there, time flew by in a blur of discovery and lessons from the lens, camaraderie, and laughter. Between their adventures, Maya Patel encouraged them to mingle nature with photography, reminding Lara of the responsibilities that came with capturing its essence.

"You have the power to spark change, Lara," Maya said steadily. "Each photograph is a testament to a story–the beauty and fragility of the world. What will your lens reveal?"

Feeling imbued with purpose, Lara nodded, each adventure emboldening her as she aligned her passion with advocacy. Her camera was now a bridge between her love for nature and a newfound desire to protect it.

As darkness settled around them like a soft cloak, the weight of their collective stories enveloped the evening. Archie Bramwell, the historian, had shared tales of ancient ruins, each sunset igniting Lara's love for history's whispers.

"Remember," he'd said, "underneath the layers of time are voices longing to be heard. Capture every moment, and you may just uncover new paths."

REFLECTIONS ON THE ROAD: LESSONS FROM THE LENS

And so, as they gathered under the stars on their last night of this leg of their journey, Lara reflected on the road they'd travelled. She had become an artist of life itself, each lesson imprinted in her heart: the value of patience taught by Theo, the thrill of adventure woven by Scarlett, the insights from Jasper, and the environmental wisdom offered by Maya, all curated through the lens of her camera.

Lara felt a gentle swell of gratitude. Through the simple act of capturing, she had discovered the essence of not merely filming the world but rather embracing it—the powerful connection binding her spirit to every landscape, every smile etched on their friends' faces.

Now, as she surveyed the surrounding constellations, the freedom she had championed through each click solidified deep within her core, revealing layers of potential still waiting to be unveiled.

With a loving smile and newfound understanding, Lara aimed her camera up toward the infinite possibilities of the sky, her heart echoing the lessons from the road she'd conquered. Freedom, she realised, resided not only in the frame before her but in the stories she was yet to tell.

THE GALLERY OF MEMORIES: A WORLD OF COLOUR

The sun dipped low in the sky, casting a golden hue across the quaint village as Lara Hargrove prepared for another journey of capture. With her camera slung across her chest, she felt the familiar surge of excitement mixed with the sweet fragrance of spring blooms. Today was not just another adventure; it was the day they would explore the place Evelyn swore was bursting with stories–the hidden corners of the village that whispered tales from years gone by.

"Are you ready, Lara?" Finn O'Reilly, her local guide and confidant, beamed with his characteristic charm. With his satchel full of sketchbooks and a map that he knew by heart, he was a walking encyclopedia of the village's secrets. "I promise, you'll want to have your finger on the shutter for this one!"

THE GALLERY OF MEMORIES: A WORLD OF COLOUR

"Absolutely!" Lara replied, her wheelchair gliding smoothly over the cobblestones as they made their way toward a pastel-coloured building–its shutters were a vibrant turquoise. "Evelyn and I have been dreaming about this!"

As they arrived at the small gallery housed within, Lara's breath caught in her throat. The sun poured through the tall windows, illuminating canvases that spoke more than mere words could convey. Each painting shimmered with passion, inviting her in with swirling colours and intricate textures.

"Welcome to the Gallery of Memories," a warm voice echoed. It belonged to Nadia Thompson, the seasoned travel journalist who had become both a mentor and a dear friend to Lara. "I thought it was time you both saw the treasures enclosed within these walls."

"Are these all local artists?" Lara asked, her eyes darting from painting to painting, hungry for details.

Nadia nodded, a smile lighting her face. "Yes. Each piece tells a story, capturing the essence of our vibrant community and the natural world surrounding us. They've each taken the mundane and transformed it into their truth."

Just then, Theo Marquez, a wildlife photographer whose enigmatic nature captivated

Lara, entered the gallery. He carried a wrapped canvas under his arm, the edges peeking out in vivid greens and earthy browns. "Just finished one of my latest," he announced, laying it gently on an easel. The scene before them showcased a wild sunset breaking over a lush, untamed landscape, birds in joyful flight silhouetted against the melting colours.

"Wow! That's stunning," Lara murmured, snapping a quick photograph, her heart fluttering with inspiration. "What's the story here?"

"A little adventure up the coast," Theo replied, his eyes glinting with excitement. "I wanted to capture the moment when daylight kisses the earth goodnight. That fleeting glance of nature's breath–"

"Oh, I would love to see that!" Evelyn exclaimed, gesturing animatedly. "Imagine framing that sunset in a series! We could explore the coastline next time, Lara. It's perfect!"

"Yes!" Lara agreed, her mind racing with possibilities. Even as her wheelchair anchored her, her imagination soared freely, painting pictures without barriers.

Emilio Cruz, the tech-savvy inventor, arrived shortly after, lugging what seemed like a large suitcase. "I come bearing gifts!" he declared, sliding the case open to unveil a custom camera rig tailored specifically for Lara. "You're going to love this. It'll allow you to shoot at new angles without worrying about stability. You'll have a whole new world of perspectives to play with."

"Emilio, you're a genius!" Lara exclaimed, overwhelmed with gratitude. She could hardly comprehend the technology he'd created for her, but the spark of excitement was undeniable. This would enhance her ability to capture moments, to see life from different views and articulate her adventures more vividly.

"Let's try it out!" Finn suggested, eyes twinkling with mischief. "There's a beautiful park just around the corner that I think holds many stories—I know the owner!"

They left the gallery, venturing back to the outdoors that filled with laughter and the scent of blooming wisteria hanging heavy in the warm air. Lara's spirit soared; each click of her shutter unveiled a world of shimmering colours, stories encapsulated in milliseconds.

As they moved through the park, filled with majestic trees draped in a carpet of blossoms, Lara felt the harmony of life echoing her own journey. She spotted an elderly gentleman seated under a sprawling oak, feeding a flurry of birds that danced around him. It clicked—it was Jasper Woodson!

"Mr Woodson!" she called out, wheeling closer as the others followed. He looked up, a glint of recognition sparkling in his eyes.

"Ah, young Miss Hargrove! Come to capture my good side, have you?" he chuckled, his voice reminiscent of a rolling brook. The warmth of their friendship enveloped Lara, filling her heart with joy.

"More like your stories, if you're willing to share them," she replied.

Jasper gestured with gnarled hands, his smile breaking through the lines on his weathered face. "Stories, indeed. Just as a photograph captures a moment, a story captures a life. Would you like to hear of my younger days exploring art and acknowledging the beauty in the forgotten?"

She nodded eagerly, snapping pictures of the exuberant birds dancing about him while he shared tales of adventures, each word steeped in nostalgia. Shadows and sunlight played around them, framing Jasper perfectly in a glittering memory that Lara would never tire of.

As the afternoon light began fading, Scarlett Rivers, the extreme sports enthusiast, zipped into view, her energy electric. "I heard there's an adventure brewing! Who's up for some cliff-top photography at sunset?"

The invitation sent a shiver of excitement through Lara. "Count me in!" she exclaimed, the thrill of spontaneity igniting her pulse.

"Let's go!" Finn cheered, and they all rallied together, united in newfound enthusiasm. The group wheeled and strolled toward the ledges, chattering between bursts of laughter as they prepared for the adventure that awaited.

Upon reaching the cliffs, the view unfolded like a masterpiece. High above the world, Lara set her camera to capture the breathtaking panorama—the hues of the sunset igniting the sky with violets, pinks, and golds spilling onto the horizon.

"Emilio's rig!" Lara barely managed to utter, the words tumbling free as she positioned herself for the perfect shot. She leaned into the beauty of the moment, her heart synchronized with the rhythm of nature, feeling more alive than ever.

As the sun dipped lower, casting long shadows, Lara aimed her lens towards the fading light that caressed their surroundings. Click. The image forever captured in time, blending the vibrancy of colour with the camaraderie of friendship.

"What do you see?" Theo asked quietly beside her, eyes locked onto her camera's viewfinder.

"Freedom," she replied, blinking away the emotion swelling in her chest. "Freedom in every snapshot; the laughter, the stories, the colours."

A knowing smile spread across Theo's face. He understood. Just as his wildlife photography had unveiled nature's beauty to the world, Lara's lens was a portal—a door to new perspectives.

As the evening drew on, the sky darkened, dotted with glimmering stars; each one shone with the stories they'd shared that day, their vibrant colours woven into the tapestry of their lives. It was then Lara realised her journey transcended the physical act of photography. It had become a masterpiece of moments—of laughter, adventure, and the love that surrounded her.

"I want everyone to experience this," she declared, the fire of determination ignited within her. "These stories need to be framed and shared. Each memory, every colour—becoming part of the gallery of life."

"Then let's do it together," Evelyn embraced Lara warmly. "The world is waiting for it!"

As her friends cheered in agreement, Lara felt the essence of what she had sought—freedom through connection, captured forever within the gallery of memories they were building together.

And so, in that moment, Lara Hargrove realized that the camera was not merely her tool; it was the key to unlock and share the boundless beauty in a world rich with colours, laughter, and unbridled adventures.

A BRUSH WITH FREEDOM: FINDING MY VOICE

The sun hung low in the sky, casting a golden hue across the sprawling landscape. Lara Hargrove felt a tingling excitement in her fingertips as she positioned her camera, her weapon of choice, and readied herself for another adventure. This time, she had chosen the rugged cliffs overlooking the breathtaking shoreline, where the waves crashed violently against the rocks with a ferocity that mirrored her own restless spirit.

"Ready for a wild one, Lara?" Finn O'Reilly, her ever-enthusiastic guide, flashed her a cheeky grin as he leaned against a weathered stone wall, his arms crossed. The light played tricks with the shadows, accentuating the rugged features of his face. Finn had an endless supply of stories about this place; every nook and cranny held a secret, and Lara was determined to capture them.

"As ready as I'll ever be," she replied, a spark igniting within her. With each outing, her confidence in manoeuvring her camera, and her wheelchair, had grown tremendously, thanks to the support of her friends and the thrilling explorations they shared.

"Let's get those waves crashing in the frame," he urged, lifting her spirits even higher. A laugh escaped Lara's lips, a delightful sound that marked her renewed sense of freedom.

With skilled hands, she adjusted the lens, focusing intently. It was here, amidst the raw beauty of nature, that Lara felt most at peace. The camera became an extension of her gaze, and she welcomed the stories trapped in every frame, eager to unveil them. Among the hills and valleys—those natural canvases—she found her voice. And as the camera shutter clicked, reality transformed into a tapestry woven from shadows and light.

"What about that angle?" Finn pointed to an ancient tree twisted by wind and time at the edge of the cliffs—its branches extended like decrepit fingers reaching into the sky.

"Perfect!" Lara shouted back, her pulse quickening. She manoeuvred her chair towards the magnificent old tree, its gnarled trunk speaking tales of resilience and survival that resonated with her journey. Here she was, a young woman living life on her own terms, daring to live past any limitations life had thrust upon her.

With the aid of her friends, Lara had explored remarkable places—each photograph a testament to her courage and growth. Evelyn's unwavering support had not only helped Lara frame her adventures beautifully but had also sparked creativity within her. After each outing, they would gather to sort through the day's captures, laughing and reliving enchanting moments together.

"Maya would love this spot!" Finn exclaimed, nudging Lara out of her concentration. "The coastline is stunning, isn't it? Think of the advocacy work she could do here!"

Lara felt a surge of excitement at the thought. Maya Patel, the passionate environmentalist, had drawn her in not just to appreciate nature but to fight for its preservation. A wave of responsibility washed over her as she realised her photographs could help to tell the stories of those spaces most in danger.

"Let's do it, Finn! Capture a moment that tells the story," Lara declared, determined to align her craft with a purpose.

After adjusting the settings on her camera, she aimed to capture more than just beauty; she wanted to touch lives through her images, becoming an advocate for the environment while also embracing the wild spirit of adventure she'd discovered within herself.

The crashing waves echoed the turmoil she had faced–fears of inadequacy and the crushing weight of self-doubt. But here, on this splendid cliff, she was finally beginning to conquer them.

"Do you hear that?" Finn asked, tilting his head. The information of his local tales blended with Lara's desire to narrate her own. It reawakened the energy within her; she could almost feel every important moment waiting to be captured and preserved.

Lara instinctively turned her lens toward the tumultuous sea, capturing the mighty waves as they crashed against the rocks, their energy resonating like a heartbeat in her chest. Each clap of sound spoke freedom; every spray of water splashed against her aspirations. She pivoted slightly as the tableau of nature unfolded into a beautiful portrait with the intensity of the ocean just being mesmerising.

"More vibrant colours, Lara! Let them shine!" she heard Evelyn's voice in her mind. The thought propelled her to adjust the settings further. She hit the shutter button again and again until she was certain she'd framed true magic.

As she scrutinised the images on her screen, Theo Marquez, the enigmatic wildlife photographer, appeared on the scene, drawn by the same pulse of inspiration that coursed through the air. "What a fierce coast!" he mused aloud, fingers brushing through his curls, a thoughtful look in his eyes as he regarded her handiwork. "Capture the wild spirit that embodies this place, Lara. Don't just frame it; become a part of it."

Lara nodded, grateful for his encouragement. His own work often found voices in the soft whispers of nature through the lens, and she understood now that she was learning to dance between the frames—creating an intimate dialogue with the world she was learning to love.

"Where's your next shot?" Theo asked, genuinely intrigued.

"Right here! I want to tell their story," she replied, gesturing to the waves as they receded, leaving behind glistening patterns on the rocks that looked as if nature had painted them with an artist's brush.

The sun began to dip below the horizon, and Lara could sense it was more than just a sunset; it was an invitation. It beckoned her to embrace every fleeting moment, and suddenly she wanted nothing more than to infuse her photographs with the freedom she felt inside.

By the time they broke for a quick lunch at a nearby café, her spirit soared. Evelyn animatedly recounted tales of their previous adventures, with Scarlett's wild antics emerging as the climax of their banter. As they exchanged laughter over warm drinks, Lara's heart swelled with gratitude. The camaraderie bubbled over, revitalising her determination.

"The stories we create, Lara, they matter," Evelyn said, nudging their friend with affection. "You're not just taking pictures; you're capturing our lives, our journeys."

Maya soon joined them, her energy contagious. "I can see the passion in your work, Lara. You're framing freedom; you're telling the world to take notice!" she said with a twinkling smile.

"Let's push it further!" Scarlett cheered, clapping her hands. "Seek out the extreme angles! The daring shots!" With every word, Lara's resolve tightened; she yearned to push the boundaries of her craft, to explore depths she had yet to discover through her lens.

After lunch, they decided to take a long walk along the beach, reveling in the bond they were strengthening with every step. It was there, between the laughter and the sound of the waves, that Lara caught sight of an old man sitting on a weathered rock, staring pensively into the depths of the sea. Intrigued, she rolled closer.

The old man, Jasper Woodson, had a weathered face but eyes filled with stories. As if sensing her curiosity, he began to speak. "Every crash of the wave is a memory, child. Each one is a moment in time—yet fleeting. You must learn to capture the ones that take your breath away."

Lara's pulse quickened at his words, feeling the weight of wisdom resonating within her. Filling her viewfinder with a heartfelt expression of the old man, she pressed the shutter; she was framing more than just his visage; she was immortalising his spirit.

As twilight descended, casting soft hues of pink and lavender across the sky, Lara knew they had struck a chord. The adventure that began as a journey for beauty had morphed into a quest for meaning—a pursuit for voice—a statement of existence through art. The artist in her now sang harmoniously with the world, narrating her story and letting it intertwine with every encounter along the way.

In that moment, Lara realised true freedom was not merely an open road or vast landscape. It was about finding her voice through the lens, a powerful commitment to capture not just beauty, but the stories that demanded to be told. What awaited her next was not just another snap; it was an entire world yearning to be framed—a world in need of a storyteller willing to embrace the wild dance of existence.

With her camera ready, she was no longer just capturing. She was living. And with every click, she was letting the world see her voice unfold.

BEYOND BORDERS: TRAVEL TALES THROUGH GLASS

The sun began its lazy descent, casting a golden hue over the historic city of Alhambra, painting its ancient walls with warmth and promise. From her vantage point in a quaint café, Lara Hargrove admired the way the light danced across the intricate tiles, each one whispering secrets of centuries past. In her lap rested her camera, a steadfast companion in her journey of discovery.

"Ready for another adventure?" Finn O'Reilly, her dashing local guide, flashed a grin that made her heart flutter with excitement. His tales of the city's hidden corners were the stuff of dreams, and today promised to unveil another layer of Alhambra's beauty.

Lara nodded, fingers itching to capture the magic that surrounded her. "Where to next?"

"We're heading to the winding streets of the old town," he replied, pushing her wheelchair with grace and ease, as if they were gliding through the very stories embedded in the cobblestones.

As they rolled through the avenues, the scent of spices filled the air, each stall an explosion of colour and life. Lara's eyes lit up as she spotted a vendor selling vibrant textiles that seemed to shimmer against the rustic backdrop. She lifted her camera, adjusting the lens to focus closely. "I want to get the details—the weaves, the textures," she said, her enthusiasm infectious.

"Good idea. Let's make sure to catch the play of light on those colours," Finn encouraged, momentarily pausing to let her frame the shot.

With each click of the shutter, Lara felt her spirit soar, as if she were flying above the boundaries of her wheelchair. She was no longer limited; she was an explorer, and the world was her canvas.

Later, they found themselves on a rooftop terrace, overlooking the sprawling landscape. Here, amidst the backdrop of mountains, Lara felt the weight of the world lifting. The sun began to set, casting an ethereal glow that contrasted beautifully with the shadows of the historic structures below.

"This is my favourite view in the entire city," Finn shared, his voice barely above a whisper. "There's a saying that to truly experience something, you must embrace it wholeheartedly. Feel the essence."

With Finn's words resonating in her mind, Lara adjusted her camera to a wider angle, determined to encapsulate the vastness of the moment. She snapped a series of shots, blending the vibrant, dimming sky with the silhouettes of the buildings, capturing the beauty of both the city and her burgeoning confidence.

"Look at this!" Lara exclaimed, showing Finn a photo she had just taken.

He grinned, leaning in to admire her work. "Absolutely stunning! You have a way of framing the world that makes it come alive."

At that moment, Evelyn Baxter, Lara's fiercely loyal best friend, skidded to a halt beside them, her eyes wide with awe. "Did you see that?" She pointed towards the rising silhouette of a majestic eagle soaring above the mountains. "A fantastic subject for your next shot, Lar!"

With no hesitation, Lara swung her camera up once more, tracking the bird. The pulse of exhilaration thrummed through her veins as she captured the fleeting moment, a blend of freedom and nature intertwining in her lens.

"Excellent timing!" Finn cheered, his voice wrapping around her like a warm embrace.

Evenings spent with Evelyn often morphed into storytelling sessions under the stars, where they would share their dreams and aspirations. Tonight, however, they found themselves poring over Lara's collection of photographs. Evelyn's artistic flair added layers of creativity to Lara's work, guiding her in framing tales that transcended mere images.

"Consider focusing on the emotions you evoke. A photograph should tell a story, right?" Evelyn suggested, flipping through pages of their adventures.

"I know!" Lara replied, a gleam of inspiration lighting her features. "It's not just about capturing sights but the feelings experienced in those moments."

The following day brought new encounters; driving through lush landscapes brought them to a sanctuary that echoed with the wild music of nature. Theo Marquez, a wildlife photographer shrouded in mystery, greeted them warmly. His passion for the untamed world was evident in the way he effortlessly moved through the tall grass, keenly aware of his surroundings.

"Stay low," he instructed, kneeling beside a patch of wildflowers. "Foxes often dart through just around this bend. Patience is key–let the world unfold before you."

Lara knelt beside him, the earth cool against her palms, feeling the pulse of nature vibrate through her. It wasn't merely an observation but an active relationship. With a cautious eye, she waited. The thrill of potential washed over her, as she captured the fleeting silhouettes darting amongst the trees.

"You've got an innate connection with nature, Lara," Theo commented, his tone thoughtful. "Your lens sees into the soul of moments."

That afternoon, they stumbled upon Jasper Woodson, the eccentric local who lived in a whimsical cottage adorned with trinkets collected from his travels. His stories of the world beyond Alhambra mesmerised Lara, weaving tales of far-flung places and vibrant cultures.

"Every corner of the world holds a tale," he said, gesturing animatedly. "When you photograph, you become a storyteller, aware of every stitch in the tapestry of life."

Inspired, Lara asked, "What's your most cherished story?"

"A night in Egypt, under a star-studded sky," he replied, eyes twinkling with nostalgia. "I clicked a photograph of a man under the pyramids, utterly lost in thought."

With a spark of creativity igniting within her, Lara realised that every shot she took would be a story waiting to be told—one that transcended borders and connected souls.

Over the next few days, the group ventured into the rugged mountains, where Lara met Scarlett Rivers, the bold extreme sport enthusiast. "You've got the heart of an adventurer," Scarlett remarked, strapping on her climbing gear. "Now, it's time to capture the adrenaline rush! Follow my lead!"

Lara couldn't help but feel invigorated as they scaled cliffs, her camera documenting every leap and bound. The thrill coursed through her veins, each heartbeat echoing the excitement of the moment.

With every adventure, they ventured deeper into the heart of nature, becoming part of the tapestry of stories that framed their journey. Lara's portfolio expanded—a visual anthology of her discoveries, moments captured through the lens of her camera.

Midway through their travels, they met Maya Patel, whose passion for the environment resonated deeply within Lara. "This is more than just photography," Maya said, urgency lacing her voice. "You have the power to ignite change through your art. Help me raise awareness about wildlife conservation."

Lara felt a shift in her journey; it was no longer just about personal expression but also the stories that held the weight of responsibility. "Yes, let's document the endangered species—bring their plight into focus," she replied, determination coursing through her.

Maya's connection fascinated her, and soon enough, every click became a document—each picture turning into a plea for nature, adding purpose to their travels.

With every face and tale woven into her growing narrative, Lara came to understand that her adventures were more than mere travel; they were opportunities for connection, for embracing the vastness of the world beyond her temporary confines.

As their expedition culminated in the ancient ruins with Archie Bramwell, the history enthusiast, Lara marvelled at how far she had come. Standing amongst the remnants of history, she began to comprehend the true essence of freedom: connecting with the world through her lens, creating stories that transcended time.

As dusk settled around them, Lara took a breath filled with sheer gratitude. Her journey, framed through adventures, had opened her eyes to life beyond borders, teaching her that every photograph bore witness to her newfound freedom.

Under the sprawling sky, she raised her camera one last time, capturing the embrace of dusk as it swallowed the ruins whole—a testimony that freedom existed not only within the confines of space, but within each moment lived, each story shared.

THE HEARTBEAT OF A CITY: URBAN EXPLORATIONS

The morning sun spilled golden light across the streets, illuminating the intricate tapestry of urban life. Lara Hargrove adjusted her camera strap, seated comfortably in her wheelchair, her heart racing with anticipation. Today, alongside Finn O'Reilly, her charming guide who seemed to know every cobblestone and alleyway, she would discover the heartbeat of the city.

"Ready?" Finn grinned, his enthusiasm contagious.

"More than ever!" Lara replied, her eyes sparkling with excitement. She had spent hours mapping out potential locations, but Finn's expertise promised to add layers of depth to her planned journey.

Their first stop was a vibrant street market filled with an array of sights and sounds. Colourful stalls displayed a mosaic of local produce, crafts, and art. Lara's fingers itched to capture everything—the vibrant reds of ripe tomatoes, the delicate blues of handcrafted pottery, and the animated faces of vendors passionately peddling their goods.

"I hear the best stories are found in the markets," Finn declared, steering her towards a stall overflowing with exotic fruits.

Lara raised her camera, framing the scene as vendors exchanged lively banter with customers. Each click of the shutter encapsulated a narrative: a woman sharing laughter over a carton of freshly-squeezed juice, a child's wide-eyed wonder at the colourful sweets, and an elderly man reminiscing about the fruits of his youth.

"Let's try that angle over there," Finn suggested, pointing to a cluster of stalls, each brimming with its unique allure.

As Lara pivoted her wheelchair to follow, she was struck by the vibrant community surrounding her. Finn's keen insights added layers to her photos, urging her to see beyond the surface. "Every glance tells a different story," he advised, "focus on capturing that essence."

"Like this?" Lara asked, snapping a picture of a laughing woman handing a bunch of bananas to a giggling child. Finn nodded approvingly, his vibrant energy only enhancing her creative process.

With her portfolio swelling with captivating shots, it was time to head into the vibrant backstreets. Finn led the way down an alley painted with a mural of a giant octopus, its tentacles spilling over crumbling brick walls. This hidden gem pulsed with life; remnants of colourful graffiti intertwined with faded posters of concerts long past.

"Here's where the city breathes," Finn said, motioning with his hands as if bestowing magic upon the scene. "Once you're in here, you feel the art, the history, the heartbeat."

Lara could feel the rhythm electrifying her spirit. She breathed in the damp, musky smell of the alley, alive with the promise of untold stories. Finding the right angle to capture the mural, she leaned in close, only to hear a soft clanging sound echoing from a nearby workshop.

"What's that?" she asked, curiosity bubbling over.

Finn beamed. "Let's check it out! I bet there's something fascinating inside."

They approached the open doorway of a blacksmith's studio, where a burly man hammered away at his anvil. Sparks flew, capturing an array of light that danced like fireflies in the dim atmosphere.

"Mind if we take some photos?" Finn called, stepping inside.

"Not at all! Just don't get too close!" the blacksmith chuckled, wiping his brow.

Lara pointed her lens to document each stroke of the hammer, captivated by how raw determination melded iron and fire. The rhythm of his work resonated within her; it mirrored her journey—one forged through perseverance and passion.

"Just look at that!" Finn exclaimed, guiding her closer to a shelf lined with intricate metalworks. "Every piece has a story; you can see the soul of the city in craftsmanship."

After capturing that moment, they stepped back into the sunlight, where bustling city life surrounded them. Lara scanned the street replete with pedestrians, street performers, and artists showcasing their crafts. She pursued a juggler captivating a small audience with vibrant scarves and bemused expressions.

"Try capturing the audience's reactions," Finn suggested with a conspiratorial grin. "That laughter is infectious!"

Lara pivoted to frame both the juggler and the spellbound crowd, laughter and awe bubbling to the surface. She clicked away, clicking in sync with their joyful gasps; each shot became a slice of humanity, a testament to the city's spirit.

Next, they ventured to a dilapidated building adorned with ivy, a remnant of a once-thriving theatre. "They say this place used to be the lifeblood of the arts," Finn explained, his voice laced with reverence. "You can sense the echoes of creativity still within these walls."

Lara set her sights through her viewfinder, finding beauty hidden amid decay. Focusing on the intricacies of the twisted vines and cracked bricks, she realised how urban spaces spoke their own language—each blemish a story of resilience, each shadow a narrative longing to be told.

As dusk settled, the city transformed as lights flickered to life. Finn guided her to a rooftop vista overlooking the skyline, a panorama that seemed to awaken the very soul of the urban heart. The horizon was tinted in shades of orange and purple, the city sprawling before them in an endless sea of glimmers.

"Perfect shot right here," Finn encouraged, pointing towards a crimson sunset reflecting off the glass of skyscrapers.

Lara had never captured anything quite like it, the colours melting together in an embrace of warmth and life. She adjusted her lens, blurring the world between her and the horizon. With each click, she felt a growing sense of liberation, allowing the camera to carry her beyond her familiar boundaries.

Suddenly the chirping of birds alighted her attention, swooping past them. "Over there!" she shouted excitedly. Finn followed her gaze, suggesting, "Let's see if we can catch them against the skyline."

With a breathless thrill, Lara clicked away, her camera capturing an inadvertent poem written by nature amidst the city's cacophony.

"Look at this city," Lara exclaimed, more to herself than to Finn. "Every corner whispers stories of triumph and artistry. I never knew I could feel so... alive here."

Finn stood beside her, his eyes reflecting the city's wonders. "That's the beauty of urban exploration. Every shot frames a moment that ignites the heart and opens the mind."

As they descended the rooftop, laughter and music floated into the air, drawing them towards a nearby square where street performers celebrated with dancers and musicians. They were pulled into the vibrant world around them, adrift in the city's lively rhythm.

Lara glanced at Finn, whose eyes sparkled with excitement. "Should we?" he asked, gesturing towards the throng of revellers.

"Absolutely! This is what it's all about," she affirmed, her heart pounding with the joy of spontaneous adventure.

They dove into the festivities, snapping photographs of dancers twirling under twinkling fairy lights, and musicians pouring their souls into captivating melodies. Evelyn was right—this urban realm brimmed with artistic flair, mirroring the essence of Lara's photography.

As the evening unfurled, Lara felt enveloped in camaraderie. Each interaction, each image captured was a brushstroke on her canvas of experience, series of moments meticulously woven together in the fabric of a city alive with energy, culture, and an array of dreams waiting to be taken.

Later, as they shared a moment of respite on a bench, restless with the joy of the day's adventures, Lara turned to Finn. "Thank you for introducing me to this world. I've captured more than just images; I've framed freedom."

"Of course! You've got the spirit of a true explorer," he replied, genuine admiration in his voice.

With renewed determination, Lara glanced back at the hustle and bustle of the city. The shutter of her camera no longer just clicked; it sang. Each beat resonated within her—life through the lens had transformed from mere sightseeing to soulful explorations. She couldn't wait for tomorrow's adventure, ready to frame yet another moment of freedom and beauty through her ever-evolving lens.

DISRUPTING STEREOTYPES: PHOTOGRAPHY AS LIBERATION

As the first light of dawn crept over the horizon, Lara Hargrove felt a familiar thrill of anticipation dance in her chest. Today was different. It was more than a mere photography outing; it was a defiant statement against the mundane perceptions of the world surrounding her. Her camera, cradled carefully in her lap, shimmered with possibilities. With each click of the shutter, she would tell a story – her story.

"Let's hit the market before the crowds," Finn O'Reilly suggested, eyes alight with excitement. His enthusiasm was infectious, and it sparked a palpable energy in the air. "I know just the place – a hidden gem with the most magical colours and characters!"

With a resolute nod, Lara guided her wheelchair onto the uneven cobblestones of the village square. It was a familiar scene, yet every lens offered a new outlook. The colours of the market stalls seemed to jump from their quiet corners, a riotous array of fruits, textiles, and the fragrant aroma of spices colliding in the morning breeze. Here lay a perfect opportunity to capture the essence of life vibrating around her.

They made their way through the warm and bustling scene, emerging into the rich tapestry of the market just as it began to awaken. Lara's fingers eagerly adjusted the lens settings on her camera, an intuitive motion born of countless practice runs. Each stall was a corridor of vibrant light, each merchant a character ready for to be immortalised in her collection. She felt her heart quicken with each snap she took.

A fleeting moment caught her eye – an elderly woman selling handmade quilts, her hands expertly weaving tales into every stitch. Lara steered closer, captivated by the intricate patterns and vivid colours. She raised her camera, catching the woman's gaze.

"May I?" Lara asked, gesturing towards her quilt. The woman smiled warmly, a smile that came with an understanding that transcended words.

"Take as many as you need, dear," she replied, wrinkles crinkling around her eyes. "These stitches are filled with stories just waiting to be told."

As Lara clicked away, Finn entered into the frame, seamlessly adding context to the scene. He shared stories of the village, of the women who crafted with pride and of the spirit that pulsed through these cobblestones. It was as if the camera momentarily liberated her from her wheelchair; she was no longer seen as out of place, nor weighed down by stereotypes.

Lara felt a familiar presence beside her – Evelyn Baxter, her best friend and protector, arrived with an eager flash of exuberance. "Did you catch the woman's smile? Make sure you highlight the way her eyes light up when she talks about her craft," Evelyn advised, her artistic flair evident in her immediate appraisal.

With Finn and Evelyn on either side, Lara was buoyed by their enthusiasm. "It's incredible how the world shifts when you see it through a lens," she said, capturing shots of curious children darting between stalls, their laughter punctuating the air. "Photography is my liberation, my escape."

"What a powerful sentiment," spoke Theo Marquez, who had appeared at their side. Always enigmatic, he offered a quiet strength. "To express oneself, especially through the lens, is a rebellion against the limits others place on us."

Lara felt a connection, a kinship with Theo that seemed to transcend the boundaries of their circumstances. "How do you find your subjects?" she asked. "Is there a secret to capturing their essence?"

Theo's lips curled into a knowing smile. "You must learn not just to see, but to feel. It starts with empathy – every shot is a heartbeat, a moment temporarily suspended in your world. Your perspective is not limited; it is truly unique."

The afternoon unfolded like a blossoming flower, with each hour bursting forth in a delightful mix of colour, life, and laughter. Lara, now entirely caught in the creative whirlpool, dedicated herself to capturing stories from every angle. With her camera, she began capturing the essence of the mundane, proving that liberation wasn't merely about breaking free from visibility; it was about rewriting the narrative through her photographs.

"Look over here!" Scarlett Rivers, ever the adventurous spirit, yelled, beckoning from a distance. She stood atop a stack of vibrant crates, effortlessly balancing as she posed gracefully. "This angle is perfect for the market–the colours, the chaos!"

Lara giggled, already envisioning how Scarlett's boldness could add drama to her collection. "I want to capture you in your element!" As she adjusted her lens, Lara understood the importance of each frame beyond mere aesthetics; they represented resilience, vibrancy, and the breaking of sculpted images.

Under the scorching sun, Maya Patel, the passionate environmentalist, drew Lara into a nearby garden bursting with life, a riot of colour that seemed to leap forth. "You can capture the collaboration between man and nature," she encouraged. "There's power in their connection and stories to share!"

Lara soaked in the beauty around her, surrendering to the enchanting fragrance released by the flowers. Here, her photograph reflected not just images but messages, urging viewers to cherish the world they inhabit. After capturing their interaction with the vibrant fauna and flora, Lara paused, breathless from both the experience and the profound realisation of how photography could fuel advocacy – not only for her but for causes she firmly believed in.

"Stereotypes can shackle us unless we cast our own reflections," Nadia Thompson, the seasoned journalist, said later as they gathered in the evening light, sipping tea while the sun dipped low. "Every photograph is a chance to disrupt preconceived notions – to show that there is depth beyond the surface."

Those words resonated deeply within Lara. She knew first-hand how society often saw her through a narrow lens, often misjudging her capabilities. She seized her camera again, this time looking inward. "I want to show them that limitation is just a frame," she declared fiercely, determination radiating from her.

As dusk painted the horizon in hues of lavender and peach, Lara found herself amidst the rich stories shared by Jasper Woodson. Each tale he spun was a thread, weaving them together, teaching her about the passions born from struggle. "There's magic in the past too," Jasper said, a twinkle in his eye. "Photography provides its own history – one that can breathe life into old tales."

The camaraderie forged in that market, those gardens, and the stories exchanged in laughter created a vibrant tapestry for Lara's heart – it was that colourful freedom she craved, now firmly within her grasp.

When it finally drew to a close, Lara gazed around at her friends – each of them embodying their individuality, breaking through the barriers that the world had cluttered in front of them.

DISRUPTING STEREOTYPES: PHOTOGRAPHY AS LIBERATION

She clicked one last shot of the group, knowing it would become a testament to their journey; each face representing courage, defiance, and above all, liberation.

As the last rays of sunlight sunk behind the hills, Lara realised that through her lens, she could reshape perceptions, challenge stereotypes, and most importantly, harness her voice. Each photograph she captured was not just a glimpse of the external world; it was a window into her soul – a declaration of freedom from the constraints that had once tried to confine her.

"Let's celebrate this moment," Finn said, wrapping an arm around her shoulder as they turned back towards the bustling market. "Today, we've changed how the world sees us and how we see ourselves."

With her camera resting securely in her lap, Lara looked up at her companions, feeling a profound sense of liberty unfurling within her. "And we will keep disrupting those stereotypes, one photograph at a time."

Together, they stepped forward handcrafted in laughter and light for all the world to see.

THE CHALLENGE OF THE STORM: NATURE'S FURY

The day began with a darkened sky that loomed over the horizon, casting a brewing tempest in its wake. Lara Hargrove adjusted her grips on the wheelchair's handlebars, a sense of thrill humming in the very core of her being. She had often pursued wonders with her camera–flowers blooming in the mountains, sunsets languidly sprawling across skies–but today promised a different kind of beauty, one born from chaos.

Finn O'Reilly stood beside her, his gaze tracing the ominous clouds. "Looks like we're in for a storm," he remarked, a hearty smile playing on his lips. "But storms can be magnificent."

"Magnificent? Or perilous?" Lara shot back, a teasing glare directed at her charming guide. Yet she felt a flutter of excitement; it was exactly this kind of unpredictability that made life worthy of exploration. Evelyn Baxter ambled along a few steps behind, her camera at the ready, framing both the overcast vignette of the landscape and Lara's determined spirit.

"Come on, Lara," Evelyn urged with a spark in her voice. "The fury of nature means drama—don't you want to capture that?"

"Absolutely," Lara replied, narrowing her focus on the dazzling array of light and shadow as turbulent winds swept across the grassy knoll. Her camera felt like a bridge between herself and the world, each snap inviting her closer to exhilarating truths.

Just then, a soft rumble of distant thunder echoed through the air, prompting a riot of excitement within the group. Theo Marquez, that mysterious wildlife photographer she had met days earlier, approached with an intense glimmer in his eyes. "There's something raw about storm light," he said, "and if you want to catch nature's real fury, we better get moving."

With a course set for the cliffs that overlooked the ocean, they departed, brushing past lush shrubs swaying under the growing wind. Lara's pulse quickened with every rotation of her wheels; the approaching storm felt like a call to arms, a relentless battle between the beauty of the world and the tempest telling stories of its own.

As they reached the cliff's edge, the wind howled like a beast awakened, tugging at their clothes, making it feel as though the very earth were trying to pull them down. Lara steadied herself, clutching her camera tightly as she captured the brimming waves crashing against the rocks below. Each roar of water was both thrilling and terrifying, yet she couldn't shake the feeling that she was witnessing the world's raw artistry.

"Be careful, Lara!" Evelyn shouted over the wind, concern etching her features as she positioned herself beside Theo, readying her own camera. "It's really starting to churn out there!"

"I'm fine!" Lara replied, her voice echoing bravely through the storm. Just then, she noticed something out of the corner of her eye—a flash of brilliant pink struggling against the grey gloom. The frayed petals of a bloom clung tenaciously to the Cliffside, caught in the storm's grasp.

"Hold tight!" Theo called, his practices eye gleaming as he captured the flower amid tumultuous winds. Inspired, Lara wheeled closer, eyes trained on the flower, her camera poised. A moment later, she pressed the shutter at the exact instant a gust of wind unfurled the petals, transforming them into a living canvas of chaos and beauty.

"Yes! That's it, Lara!" Finn encouraged, his hands raised in exhilaration. "Keep going!"

But before she could respond, a blinding flash of lightning struck, momentarily seizing her focus. Nadia Thompson, the seasoned travel journalist and veteran of the stormy skies, appeared at their side, excitement visible in her vantage on the unfolding scene. "You must be ready for the conjunction of that thunder and lightning," she advised, her voice steady. "That's often where you can find the raw emotion the elements carry."

"Emotion," Lara murmured, pondering the very essence of what she sought through her art. Wasn't it about expressing the highs and lows, the serene and the wild?

Suddenly, a monstrous roar of thunder split the sky, rattling the ground beneath them. The group collectively gasped. "We need to seek shelter!" Evelyn shouted, darting towards the rock outcropping nearby, but Lara felt a magnetic pull anchoring her wheels. "Wait! Just one more shot!" she exclaimed, her heart racing with reckless determination.

The first heavy drops of rain began to pelt down, joining the winds in their tumultuous dance. Lara defied the storm; her camera encompassed both nature's beauty and its fury, framing life in a moment that felt suspended between chaos and clarity.

Jasper Woodson, wandering out from the shadows of the outcropping, hollered, "You won't believe the stories that come from storms like these! I once lived in a village where rain would howl like spirits, and—" His words faded into the clamour of nature's voice as they all focused intently on capturing the unfolding scene before them.

Each clap of thunder resonated with the beat of Lara's heart, a crescendo that made her feel invincible. She leaned forward, manoeuvring closer to the edge where the wild seas met the rocky cliff. The water erupted in white foamy sprays, darkness swirling into torrents of energy.

"Lara, you're too close!" Finn implored, racing to steady her chair, but she only smiled, her camera's shutter clicking like a metronome of creation. She felt alive in the presence of the storm, savouring the rawness of those frayed moments.

"Just a few more shots!" Lara persisted, capturing waves as they danced, breaking against the cliff's edge like vibrant brushstrokes vying for freedom against the rigid canvas of stone.

As the storm raged, Emilio Cruz suddenly emerged, his rain-soaked clothes clinging to his

THE CHALLENGE OF THE STORM: NATURE'S FURY

frame as he brandished the intricate camera rig he had built for Lara. "Lara! This is the perfect time to use it!" he shouted, beckoning her to use the apparatus he had meticulously designed.

Her eyes lit up as she saw the potential; with newfound inspiration, she manoeuvred the rig into position, and soon there was a stillness; a fleeting tranquillity amidst the storm. She took a breath, composure amidst chaos, and captured her surroundings anew—a symphony of nature's rage captured through the lens of her camera.

It seemed nature had momentarily paused to allow Lara her moment. What appeared next was no mere image but a story condensed into a frame. Each photograph she took was transformative; it was no longer just about the world outside her—it was about her own journey through adversity, filling her portfolio with snapshots of her very essence tangled with elements that spoke the truth of life.

As the storm began to recede, the sun broke through the clouds, painting the sky in brilliant hues of orange and pink, and illuminating the drenched landscape with breathtaking vibrancy. A joyous cheers erupted from the group as they embraced their accomplishment; Lara had indeed captured nature's fury—and with it, a deeper sense of freedom.

"Look!" Evelyn gestured toward the horizon. "The storm has revealed a rainbow."

"All that chaos for this," Theo mused, a proud smile gracing his lips as they gathered around Lara, sharing their triumph over the tempest.

"Together, we've framed freedom in its most authentic form," Lara proclaimed, her voice teeming with passion.

In that moment, engulfed in the glow of the dying storm and the promise of new beginnings, Lara understood that her journey was more than capturing images; it was about seizing the tempest within and embracing every shade, every hue, every chaotic turn of life that led her here.

FRAMING FREEDOM: EMPOWERMENT THROUGH ART

The dawn broke over the horizon, painting the sky in hues of coral and lavender as Lara adjusted her camera settings with fingers that trembled with excitement. This day was to be a testament to her journey—not just an exploration of the picturesque trails winding through the glen, but an exploration of the depths of her own empowerment through art. She had woken up with a fire in her belly, fuelled by dreams of dawn-lit landscapes and the hope of discovering her voice through each shot she captured.

"Are you ready for a day of magic?" Finn O'Reilly appeared beside her, his charming grin illuminating the crisp morning. He carried a rucksack filled with provisions and an infectious enthusiasm, his dark hair tousled by the morning breeze.

Lara met his gaze with a determined smile. "Absolutely. I want today to be different; I want to feel the world through my lens."

Finn nodded with a knowing glint in his eyes. "Let's find a spot that captures everything—freedom, beauty, and a hint of adventure."

With Finn's guidance, they navigated along narrow paths woven with wildflowers and ferns, each vivid petal whispering secrets of the wild to Lara. As they reached a small clearing overlooking a cascading waterfall, she felt her heart surge—this was it, her canvas of opportunity.

Lara set her camera, gingerly positioning it to frame the idyllic scene. Just as she peered through the viewfinder, Evelyn appeared, adorned in a kaleidoscope of colours that matched the vibrancy of the landscape.

"Lara, you won't believe the way the sunlight dances on the water here! It's going to make for a stunning shot." Evelyn's keen eye for beauty complemented Lara's visionary spirit.

"Hold that thought," Lara chuckled, delighting in her friend's enthusiasm. With a click of the shutter, she captured the moment, the water glistening like diamonds under the embrace of the sunlight.

As they settled on a blanket spread on the grass, their laughter melded with the sounds of nature—

the rhythmic rush of the waterfall, chirping birds, and the whisper of the wind. It was in this serene yet lively atmosphere that Lara felt empowered to express herself. With Evelyn's artistic flair and Finn's storytelling charm, she began to conceptualise her photographs not just as images, but as vessels carrying the essence of her adventures.

"Do you remember Jasper?" Evelyn asked between bites of a sandwich. "He has a myriad of tales. I've been thinking… we could weave those stories into your photographs. What do you think?"

"Stories… woven with images." Lara mused aloud, her mind racing through possibilities. "That could infuse the pictures with a depth I hadn't considered. Each snap could be a doorway to history, capturing the fleeting moments that are often overlooked."

Their thoughts blossomed like the wildflowers around them, each idea taking root and intertwining with the next. But the thrill of creation quickly turned into a rush of apprehension as Lara recalled the challenges that lay ahead.

"Sometimes, I worry I won't capture the essence of what I see," she admitted, her gaze lowering to the grass.

"Lara, remember, it's not about perfection." Finn's voice was steady, filled with warmth. "It's about your perspective— your unique story. What you capture through your lens is inherently yours. That's what makes it beautiful."

His encouragement wrapped around her like a comforting embrace, filling her with renewed vigour. A newfound determination surged within, and Lara decided to explore even further—embracing each moment as it arrived, focusing on the narratives unfurling all around.

As the afternoon unfolded, the trio ventured deeper into the woods, where the dense foliage formed a natural cathedral of green, sunlight filtering through the leaves like golden threads. There, they stumbled upon the enigmatic figure of Theo Marquez, who lay flat on the ground, his camera poised like a sniper, hunting stories amongst the wild.

"What are you capturing?" Lara asked, her curiosity piqued as she wheeled closer.

"The delicate movement of these butterflies," Theo replied, his voice both serene and intense. "Every flutter tells a story, don't you think?"

Lara watched in awe as he sprang to his feet after a successful shot. "I'll teach you. It's not just about the shots you take but how deeply you connect with your subjects."

There was beauty in every frame, and Theo showed Lara how to see even the smallest details in life— the shimmering wings of a butterfly, the gentle ripple of water. Each detail transformed into a canvas, rich with stories waiting to be told.

Inspired by her new mentor, Lara felt the weight of the world lift off her shoulders. The forest's whispers told her there was freedom in capturing the essence of the moment, that each click of her camera could echo her own transformation.

Their adventure continued, leading them to the vibrant colours of a street festival in the village where Jasper resided. The atmosphere was electric, crowds swirling with laughter and joy. Jasper regaled the group with tales of history and community, his words spinning directly into the heart of Lara's photography.

"Every face has a story," he exclaimed, pointing to an elderly man selling hand-painted pots under a vibrant umbrella. "Capture that life! Find the soul in their gaze."

Excited and emboldened, Lara navigated through the crowd, her camera ready to seize the vibrant tapestry of life around her. With every click, she noticed how her confidence grew, her surroundings morphing into a gallery of emotions—people laughing, children playing, artists passionately showcasing their craft.

Suddenly, amidst all this, Lara spotted Scarlett Rivers zipping past on her skateboard, the embodiment of boldness and freedom. Inspired, Lara shifted her viewpoint to capture the dynamic motion, freezing the exhilarating energy in a single frame.

"There you are, charming the world again, Lara!" Scarlett exclaimed, her hair flowing behind her like a comet as she skidded to a stop. "Join me! Feel the rush of adrenaline, and let's take this adventure to new heights!"

Lara's heart raced at the thought, and with each passing moment, she realised that every photo she took was a testament to her journey–her embrace of life beyond her wheelchair. She envisioned creating a photo essay, weaving together the stories of people, nature, and history, reflecting resilience and freedom in tandem.

That evening, as the sun dipped below the horizon, staining the sky with hues of gold and purple, Lara gathered her newfound friends around a fire. The night was alive with the crackle of wood and the laughter of adventurers, their stories intertwining like of a glorious tapestry.

"Lara, your pictures resonate; they echo the beauty of what you experience," Nadia remarked, her voice warm against the gentle hum of the night. "You're not just a photographer–you're a storyteller and an advocate. Share these narratives with the world."

A wave of joy surged through Lara. As she reflected on their day—the stunning colours of life woven into stories and laughter—the world began to feel limitless. Art had become her conduit, transforming her feelings of confinement into bursts of creativity, empowerment radiating within every frame she created.

As the fire's glow illuminated their faces, Lara realised that her journey was just beginning. With her camera as her ally, she could channel her spirit into art—frames that would echo with the resonance of freedom, colour, and stories untold, capturing the essence of life itself.

Her heart brimming with gratitude, Lara pondered the narratives yet to unfold, ready to embrace every opportunity to chase the beautiful, uncharted territories through the lens of her camera. Each photograph, a step towards liberation; every moment, a chance to be alive.

In that circle of warmth and camaraderie, she silently vowed that she would frame her freedom through art, sharing her journey with the world, one enchanting photograph at a time.

A JOURNEY'S END: THE FINAL SHOT OF LIBERATION

As dawn broke over the horizon, the golden hues of sunlight spilled across the landscape, painting the world in a soft glow that beckoned Lara Hargrove to rise to the occasion. Today was a defining moment, the culmination of her journey through the lens—a journey of discovery, self-realisation, and liberation.

Lara adjusted her camera settings, her heart thrumming with excitement. This was more than just another photograph; it was the final shot that would encapsulate everything she had learned and become. The air was crisp, and the scent of dew-kissed grass filled her lungs, mingling with the comforting aroma of the fresh bakeries in the village below, where her adventure had truly begun.

A JOURNEY'S END: THE FINAL SHOT OF LIBERATION

Evelyn Baxter, her ever-spirited best friend, arrived with a broad grin and a steaming cup of coffee in hand. "Ready to capture your masterpiece, Ms Hargrove?" she teased, raising an eyebrow in mock seriousness.

"Absolutely! Just wait until you see what I've got planned," Lara replied, her eyes sparkling with resolve. As Evelyn pulled out her sketchbook, Lara took a moment to appreciate their bond—the laughter-laden discussions that had floated through their days, the spirited debates over angles and lighting. They had not only framed photographs; they had forged a lasting friendship through art.

Finn O'Reilly, the charming guide who had opened doors to undiscovered corners of beauty, arrived soon after. "You lot look like artists on a mission!" he called out, his mischievous glint igniting a familiar sense of adventure.

"Out here, we definitely are!" Lara called back.

Together, they rolled towards the edge of a sprawling meadow dotted with wildflowers, where they had decided to shoot the final image. The view was breathtaking; rolling hills kissed the sky, a palette of greens and yellows bursting alive with the promise of spring. Lara could almost hear the whispers of the stories etched in the landscape, tales waiting to be revealed within her frame.

"Let's not forget Theo," Evelyn reminded them playfully.

"Of course, how could I?" Lara grinned, recalling the mysterious wildlife photographer's captivating presence. His insight had deepened her connection to nature, teaching her the rhythms of the wild. Just a few days before, as they had ambled through a dense forest, he had shared his wisdom—a gentle reminder that capturing a moment often meant being present, still, and observant.

They settled into the vibrant meadow as Theo bobbed over the hill, his enigmatic smile revealing a spark of enthusiasm. "You've chosen a magnificent spot," he mused, surveying the canvas laid before them. Instead of merely commanding the landscape, Lara felt at one with it.

"Today, I want to capture the essence of freedom—the feeling that resonates deep within when you're at peace with the world," she explained, her voice steady with conviction.

Theo nodded appreciatively. "That's a worthy pursuit," he said, adjusting his own camera. "And don't forget to chase the light. It's a magnificent partner in the artistry of photography."

With her heart dancing at the possibilities, Lara began her careful composition. As she adjusted the camera, she recalled the many stories woven through her journey—the chance encounter with Jasper Woodson, the eccentric storyteller who had ignited her love for the local lore, and the thrill from spending evenings with Scarlett Rivers, whose fearless pursuit of adventure had inspired her willingness to embrace risks.

"Remember the time we tried those extreme angles down by the cliff's edge?" Evelyn laughed, recalling the moment vividly.

"Let's never forget my mild panic at that moment!" Lara quipped, her laughter harmonising with that of her friends.

Lara peered through the lens and exhaled deeply, sifting through the beautiful chaos of the scene before her. She was reminded of the impacts of conservation from Maya Patel's fervent pleas for protecting endangered habitats, her words echoing in Lara's mind. Each petal, every flutter of a bird, every ripple of the breeze—each detail illuminated by the purpose to protect the world's beauty pulsed through Lara's heart.

"Okay, everyone," she called out, positioning herself low and adjusting the aperture. "This is it!"

The click of the shutter became a heartbeat, echoing deeper than mere photography. It represented a symphony of personal growth, the melding of bravery and uncompromising passion. It was her liberation.

Suddenly, as if responding to her call, a majestic hawk soared above, silhouetted against the dawn sky. The sun glinted off its wings, and in that moment, as she pressed the shutter, everything crystallised.

"Got it!" Lara exclaimed, a rush of euphoric excitement washing over her. She knew she had captured more than just an image; she had encapsulated her journey, her struggles, and ultimately, her triumph.

Finn let out a whoop of joy. "That was stunning, Lara! You're a natural!"

Theo nodded in agreement. "Your perspective is unique; you've grown tremendously."

Feeling the vibrations of their praise, Lara beamed.

Evelyn reached over, clasping Lara's hand firmly. "Do you remember when we first started this trip, when you feared you would miss out on life? Look how far you've come! This final shot is not just a reflection of what's outside, but what's within you."

Lara was overwhelmed. Every step she had taken—each adventure, each challenge faced—had led her to this moment of clarity. It was no longer about the limitations society imposed upon her; it was about the capability that lay within herself.

A JOURNEY'S END: THE FINAL SHOT OF LIBERATION

Even as they celebrated this pivotal shot, time seemed to pause, allowing Lara a moment for reflection. She thought of Nadia Thompson, whose mentorship had been invaluable, igniting in her a passion for storytelling through art. The lessons they'd shared would forever linger in the soft touch of the shutter button.

Lara felt ready to step away from the lens and into a narrative of her own, where she no longer needed to seek validation from others. The world was her canvas, and she was the artist.

With Evelyn, Finn, Theo, and the vivid tapestry of experiences dancing in her mind, she felt something shift. The final shot was simply a metaphor for the bravery within her—a liberation that transcended the physical and plunged into the depths of her very spirit.

"Shall we do one more, just for good measure?" Lara asked, her voice brimming with newfound confidence.

"Absolutely!" the group cheered, eager to indulge in one last moment with her.

Together, they posed, laughter echoing through the meadow as they celebrated the culmination of a journey that had reshaped them all. Behind the lens, Lara pressed the shutter once more, not for the image, but for the joyous connection of friendship—an everlasting bond framed within the lens of liberation.

As the sun climbed higher, casting light across the vibrant scene, it illuminated their laughter, their struggles, and their shared pursuit of beauty.

Today marked not just a journey's end, but the beginning of an extraordinary path carved by the lens of her camera—one filled with endless possibilities, adventures waiting to unfold, and stories yearning to be captured, both behind the lens and beyond.

FINAL FRAME: THE ESSENCE OF FREEDOM

As the sun dipped beneath the horizon, casting a golden glow across the landscape, Lara Hargrove positioned her camera, taking a moment to breathe in the beauty she had so fervently sought. The panorama of rolling hills, vibrant wildflowers, and a sky splashed with hues of pink and orange unfolded before her—an endless canvas, much like the journey she had undertaken.

"Look at that light," Finn whispered, his voice low and reverent beside her. "It's as if the world is smiling just for you."

With a flick of her wrist, Lara adjusted the settings on her custom rig, a marvel of Emilio's invention that allowed her boundless freedom to manoeuvre. This was not just a camera; it was her lifeline, her voice. With each click, she had woven stories that transcended her limitations, turning moments into memories and challenges into triumphs.

Evelyn, ever the cheerleader, leaned over her shoulder. "This one's going to be something special, Lara. I can feel it." Together, they shared a knowing smile, an unspoken understanding that the journey had forged bonds much deeper than mere friendship.

Theo approached, a hint of awe in his eyes. "It's not just the landscape that captivates. It's how you see it—how you frame it. You've become part of the very essence of what you capture."

With a shake of her head, Lara felt the weight of gratitude wash over her. From Jasper's tales of yore to Scarlett's daredevil escapades, from Nadia's wisdom to Maya's passionate activism—each encounter, each laugh and every obstacle had been a brushstroke on the canvas of her life, painting a vivid tableau of resilience and hope.

As they gathered around for one final reflection, Archie recalled a piece of history that resonated deeply, "Every great work of art carries a story. Your photographs, Lara, are a testament—a legacy for those who dare to see beyond what's visible."

With one last glance at the sun slipping into twilight, Lara raised her camera. This would be her last shot, the culmination of every adventure, every

FINAL FRAME: THE ESSENCE OF FREEDOM

fleeting moment that had shaped her spirit. She snapped the photo, capturing the gentle embrace of dusk, the laughter of friends, and the promise of more journeys yet to come.

"Here's to framing freedom!" she proclaimed, her voice ringing with exhilaration.

As the soft click of the shutter echoed in the dusk, Lara knew she had not only framed her world but redefined it, breaking free from the confines she once thought held her captive. In that moment, with her friends by her side, she felt the true essence of independence—a freedom found not just in the adventures she embarked upon, but in the stories she would continue to tell through her lens.

And so, as the stars began to twinkle above, Lara Hargrove rolled forward, the horizon vast and inviting—her camera in hand, her heart ablaze, knowing that the journey was far from over, and the world remained wide open, awaiting her next adventure.